The Station

Also by Keira Andrews

Contemporary

Honeymoon for One
Beyond the Sea
Ends of the Earth
Arctic Fire
The Chimera Affair

Holiday
Only One Bed
Merry Cherry Christmas
The Christmas Deal
Santa Daddy
In Case of Emergency
Eight Nights in December
If Only in My Dreams
Where the Lovelight Gleams
Gay Romance Holiday Collection

Sports
Kiss and Cry
Reading the Signs
Cold War
The Next Competitor
Love Match
Synchronicity (free read!)

Gay Amish Romance Series
A Forbidden Rumspringa
A Clean Break
A Way Home
A Very English Christmas

Valor Duology
Valor on the Move
Test of Valor
Complete Valor Duology

Lifeguards of Barking Beach
Flash Rip
Swept Away (free read!)

Historical

Kidnapped by the Pirate
Semper Fi
The Station
Voyageurs (free read!)

Paranormal

Kick at the Darkness
Kick at the Darkness
Fight the Tide

Taste of Midnight (free read!)

Fantasy

Barbarian Duet
Wed to the Barbarian
The Barbarian's Vow

The Station

by Keira Andrews

The Station
Written and published by Keira Andrews
Cover by Dar Albert
Second Edition

Copyright © 2018 by Keira Andrews
First edition published 2010

All rights reserved. This book or any portion thereof may not be reproduced or used in any manner whatsoever without the express written permission of the author or publisher except for the use of brief quotations in a book review.

ISBN: 978-1-988260-28-0
Print Edition

This is a work of fiction. Names, characters, businesses, places, events and incidents are either the products of the author's imagination or used in a fictitious manner. No persons, living or dead, were harmed by the writing of this book. Any resemblance to any actual persons, living or dead, or actual events is purely coincidental.

Acknowledgements

Thanks to Anara and Leta for their assistance and friendship!

Prologue

Essex, England. 1833

THE DARE HAD seemed simple enough.

Ride his father's new stallion bareback around the stable and return it to its pen, none the worse for wear. Colin's cousin, William, had issued the challenge and watched from a garden bench some yards away. The boys were at Colin's house, alone for a spell as their parents attended a funeral in the village.

Well, alone except for the servants, including the new stable master, Patrick Callahan. Colin's father had been quite reluctant to hire an Irishman, let alone one who was but twenty-two years old, yet he had relented when he witnessed Patrick's unquestionable mastery with the horses. When Colin asked why it mattered where Patrick was from, his father had told him he'd understand when he was grown.

At thirteen, Colin was quite tired of being treated as a child, although he still looked like one. William had sprouted up, and though they were the same age and Colin was months older, he remained small and spindly.

As Colin neared the stable, Patrick emerged unexpectedly. Colin stopped in his tracks, heart in his throat. He'd never spoken with Patrick before, and from a distance he seemed a stern sort of man. Patrick nodded to him. "How is the young lord today?"

"W-well. And you?" Colin stammered, his pulse racing. He'd

thought Patrick was playing cards with the groundskeepers in the shed. Colin had heard their raucous laughter drifting on the air only moments before. His austere parents were away so infrequently that everyone took advantage of their absence to engage in some sport.

"Aye, well enough." Patrick was six feet tall and lean, his muscles firm. His light brown hair complemented hazel eyes, and freckles faintly dusted his cheeks. His jaw was strong and usually rough with stubble. Colin had overheard the maids swooning over Patrick since his arrival. "Did you need something?"

"No, just going to visit Viola."

"She's a good mare. I'm sure she'll appreciate the company. I'll just be in the shed, playing a hand." He leaned down and whispered, "That'll be our little secret, all right?"

Colin nodded vigorously. He was delighted to be in Patrick's confidence and couldn't blame him for wanting to take a break from his work. As Patrick went on his way, Colin mused that the stable master was unlike anyone he had ever met. He'd never even been to London, which his parents had declared far too dirty and full of heathens. The fact that Patrick was Irish made him quite exotic.

As Colin entered the stable and approached the stallion, the happy fluttering in his belly became a churning. The animal was taller than Colin remembered, and climbing atop would prove to be quite a challenge. Although he was a fair rider, Colin had never been on a stallion, let alone bareback. He'd never even ridden Viola without a saddle. He was beginning to think he'd made an unwise decision, to say the least.

Still, he'd been dared, and he'd never backed down from a test of courage yet, even though once it had resulted in him falling from a tree and snapping his arm. He'd insisted to his parents that it had been his idea to climb, although it was William's. It always was. William was a daredevil, and Colin's pride compelled him to try his best to keep up.

After a few deep breaths, Colin approached the stallion's pen. He plucked an apple from a bucket and cautiously held it on his flat palm. The horse nipped him, but Colin didn't cry out. He murmured to the animal in what he hoped was a calming fashion and tentatively stroked its snout.

When it seemed comfortable enough with Colin's presence and was munching the fruit, Colin clambered up onto the side of the stallion's stall. He took another breath, gathering his nerve. Then another, and another. He feared he might swoon before even getting on the horse at all.

It's now or never. Patrick wouldn't play at cards all afternoon, and Colin's parents would return. Leaning over precariously, he reached for the door to the stall. He exhaled and muttered a quick prayer. Then he lifted the latch and dropped onto the horse's back, his fingers clutching its mane.

The stallion bolted, hooves pounding as it burst out of the stable. Colin dug his knees and heels into the horse's flanks, trying to steer it around the building. As he held on for dear life, he very quickly realized he didn't have the skill or power to control the stallion, certainly not without a bridle. Panic flared as he gasped for air.

Colin could hear William's faint shouts as the stallion thundered off across the meadow, but he didn't dare look back. All he could do was keep his head down and cling to the horse as it galloped away. Time seemed eternal as it ran across the grounds and continued along the river. He called for it to stop, his voice hoarse with terror, convinced of his impending demise, but the stallion had a mind of its own.

The countryside was beginning to look frighteningly unfamiliar when suddenly another set of hoofbeats approached. He heard a voice, and then in one movement, a strong arm pulled him from the horse's back as a rope looped over its neck. Colin found himself facedown over the back of Patrick's horse as Patrick yanked on the reins and brought both animals to a stop.

In one smooth motion, Patrick dismounted and put Colin on his feet. Colin was perilously close to tears, and he blinked rapidly, gasping, his heart thumping painfully. Patrick knelt in front of him and took his shoulders gently. He shook his head, clearly exasperated.

"You're all right, lad. You're damn foolish, but you're all right."

Colin struggled to catch his breath. He actually *was* all right. He was uninjured and, most remarkably, still alive. He'd never been so frightened in his life and hoped he never would be again.

"I'm impressed you stayed on. You're a natural rider. Next time, come and ask and I'll give you a more suitable horse, eh?" Patrick mussed Colin's hair lightly.

Colin nodded, amazed Patrick wasn't angry with him.

"And next time don't do whatever your cousin tells you. He's a little devil, that one." Patrick smiled, dimpling his cheek. "I should know. He reminds me of myself." He stood and glanced toward home. "Let's get you back before your parents return."

Once Patrick was in the saddle, he swung Colin up to sit in front of him. They cantered back along the river, Patrick holding the rope with the stallion in tow. As they rode, Colin found he was actually enjoying himself. He felt utterly secure with Patrick at his back, and laughed with pleasure as they moved into a gallop across the final meadow.

William paced by the stable, face pale with worry. "Colin! I thought you'd broken your neck for certain!"

Sliding from Patrick's horse, Colin grinned. "I told you I could do it."

"He would have ridden all the way to Dover if I hadn't stopped him and made him come home." Patrick winked and dismounted. He led the two horses inside.

William was shamefaced. "I shouldn't have made you do that. I'm sorry."

Colin felt oddly exhilarated by the whole experience, despite his recent terror. "It's okay, Will."

Just then the carriage could be heard on the drive. "Hurry! Let's pretend we were reading!" William hustled toward the house.

"In a moment." Colin darted inside the stable, where Patrick was brushing down the stallion. "Thank you. For rescuing me."

Patrick shrugged. "'Twas nothing. Perhaps one day you'll return the favor."

As Colin stole into the house through the back entrance, he promised himself he would.

Chapter One

1839

Tiptoeing into the large stable, Colin winced as the door closed behind him with a loud whine from the hinges. He'd have to remember to tell one of the servants to tend to it. He'd do it himself but had absolutely no idea where he'd obtain the oil.

Cautiously, he crept farther into the dim building. The horses had all been out for their exercise and now resided calmly in their stalls for the most part. As Colin passed, Viola huffed and stamped the wooden floor, probably eager to return to the pasture. Colin shushed her, scratching behind her ears.

As he moved toward the back of the stable, he listened carefully but heard nothing out of the ordinary. Just in case, Colin peeked around the corner toward the stable master's quarters.

Empty.

He sighed heavily and returned to Viola to give her an apple. After the first time he'd stumbled upon the two men three years before, Colin had avoided the stable for countless months, flushing with embarrassment every time he had even neared the building. He'd made every attempt to forget what he'd seen and—more importantly—how he'd reacted.

However Colin had now abandoned the pretense, at least in his own mind. It had taken him years to accept it, but he'd given in to his nature and had begun actively seeking out the clandestine activity, eager to witness it again.

Naturally as soon as he was looking for it, it was nowhere to be found.

Colin knew it was wrong on several levels. Patrick would surely be furious if he found out he was being spied upon. But more importantly, the act Colin craved was punishable by death. He should be disgusted by it.

Yet the very thought of it quickened his blood and stirred his manhood. It excited him like nothing else.

After the day Patrick had plucked him from the runaway stallion's back, they'd become friends of a sort. Patrick had given him riding lessons, and Colin had eagerly hung around the stables whenever he could, helping with the chores.

There had always been an air of defiance about Patrick, who treated Colin as a peer and not a master. But three years ago, Colin had discovered just how rebellious Patrick truly was. It had led Colin to destroy their friendship.

As Viola chomped through her apple core, Colin's thoughts drifted back.

Rain pelted the countryside and brought with it a relentless wind. Everyone holed up in the main house, but Colin grew restless. He was sixteen and bored of everything, particularly studying.

By late afternoon, the sky was so dark it was as if night had fallen. Colin bundled up and stole out the kitchen door, hurrying to the stable. He planned to keep Viola company, guessing she was as tired of being cooped up as he was. Perhaps Patrick could give him something to do. He loved visiting Patrick and helping with the animals whenever he could.

As he entered the stable, Colin was careful to shut the door quietly against the wind so as not to startle the animals. He opened his mouth to call a hello to Viola, but the words died in his throat.

A low moaning reached him, coming from the far side of the stable. Colin wasn't sure at first if the sound was human, and worried an animal was ill. But some instinct told him to be stealthy and keep his silence. He trod as lightly as he could, listening to the moans and gasps for breath with a strange excitement and mounting curiosity.

The stable master's quarters were in the back corner of the building at the end of a short corridor, and it seemed to Colin the noises were most likely coming from there. After gathering his courage, he peered slowly around the last stall.

His heart hammered so loudly he worried it would certainly be heard. Through the open door at the end of the corridor were two men. One braced himself against the wall, hands spread as he bent forward. The other man was Patrick, and Colin clapped his hand over his mouth as he gasped aloud. Patrick had mounted the man in the same manner Colin had seen horses mate, and Colin stared, transfixed.

Both men groaned and breathed harshly, breeches around their ankles, shirts undone and hanging loosely. Colin's own trousers were suddenly uncomfortably tight, and he fought only briefly against his urge to get a closer look. Taking the apple he'd brought for Viola, he held it out for the horse in the last stall, opening the door just enough to slip inside. He squeezed by the animal to the rear of the enclosure, holding his breath.

By stooping, Colin could see through a gap in the horizontal slats of wood. He was only ten feet from the straining men, and his pulse pounded. Colin had been informed of how babies were created by his dispassionate tutor, Mr. Wheeldon, years ago, but had never imagined what he was witnessing was possible. While William had been obsessed with girls of late, Colin had never found them of much interest outside of pleasant conversation.

But hiding in the stable, watching Patrick mate with a man he vaguely recognized as one of the groundskeepers, Colin was overcome with desire and exhilaration. Patrick slammed into the man over and over as Colin watched, rapt. It was as if the missing piece of a puzzle had finally locked into place.

Both men shone with a thin sheen of sweat, even in the chill, and they grunted with a satisfaction Colin had never experienced. He'd touched himself many times, but it had always felt strangely empty. William had told him that he thought about one of the housemaids dusting naked, but when Colin tried it, his loins remained stubbornly unmoved.

As Colin watched, Patrick reached around for the other man's member, grasping it tightly as he continued riding him. Colin silently loosened his trousers and snaked his hand inside. He was already hard as a rock, the tip of his cock wet. Biting his lip, he stroked himself, eyes glued to Patrick's round, firm buttocks, partially hidden by the ends of his shirt.

Colin drew blood from his lip as he flooded his hand with sticky seed. He hung on to the side of the stall, his entire body shuddering with release as he'd never felt before.

"What are you doing here? Lose your way?"

Colin jumped, his mind jolting back to the present as he spun around to find Patrick watching him quizzically. Colin had been rubbing himself unconsciously through his trousers as he'd remembered the stormy day three years past. Patrick's gaze flickered downward, and he raised an eyebrow in amusement. "Enjoying your horse, Lord Lancaster?"

"I... What? No! I was just..." Colin tore off his jacket and held it to his stomach. "I was giving Viola an apple. Nothing more."

Patrick smirked. "If you say so, Lord." The term he'd once bestowed without malice had become an insult.

"You know I'm not a lord at all," Colin mumbled. Colin's family was wealthy enough, but they weren't nobility.

"Could've fooled me. I'm surprised you're giving your mare the time of day. Thought you were too good now for hanging about in the muck. Shouldn't you be relaxing somewhere? Eating candies?" Patrick was being quite insolent and would never speak this way to Colin with others around. "You used to enjoy getting your hands dirty. But I suppose the apple doesn't fall far from the tree after all." He shrugged.

Colin flushed. After witnessing the encounter three years ago, he'd stopped his visits to the stable. He only came when he had to and had often tasked the household servants with collecting and returning Viola for him. He knew why Patrick thought he was now a pampered prince and too much of a snob to hang about as he once did. Yet truthfully he'd been too confused and troubled by his feelings to do anything but watch Patrick from afar.

Although he'd been coming again regularly to the stable for the last few months, Patrick was none the wiser, since Colin had hoped to catch him fornicating again and hadn't made his presence known. He'd thought about talking to Patrick and telling him the truth, but every time he considered it, he felt positively sick to his stomach.

"Can you not deign to listen to me?"

Colin had been so preoccupied with the fact that Patrick was standing but a few feet away, looking completely ravishing, that he had no idea what the man was saying. As usual, he didn't have the nerve to look Patrick in the eye and kept his gaze elsewhere. "Pardon?"

"Shouldn't you be running along to your tutor?"

Colin forced himself to look up at Patrick. "My tutor?"

"Although you're quite"—Patrick's eyes flicked downward again—"unpresentable at the moment."

Without another word, Colin fled, leaving Patrick's hearty laughter in his wake. As he hustled back to the main house, a two-story rectangular building of beige brick with a long, curving lane in front, Colin cursed himself for his foolishness. He should forget Patrick and stop embarrassing himself.

Passing a startled maid, Colin took the grand staircase in the foyer two steps at a time and was soon safely in his chambers, the door firmly closed. He buzzed from running into Patrick.

Although Patrick had cooled toward him considerably, Colin couldn't help but be exhilarated by the encounter.

After checking the clock on his mantle, Colin saw he still had twenty minutes before Mr. Wheeldon would arrive for their daily studies. He quickly shucked his trousers and stroked himself, imagining it was him Patrick had mounted that day in the stable.

At first, Colin had been so mortified by his reaction to the sight of Patrick and the groundskeeper that he hadn't touched himself for the longest time. He'd denied his feelings and avoided Patrick at all costs. And he'd tried with the lovely Katherine Crawford. Really, he had. But it was no good. Colin wanted men, and one man in particular. One man he could never have.

After spilling his seed, Colin swiftly cleaned himself and went to the drawing room to meet Mr. Wheeldon. The afternoon ticked by ever so slowly as they went over Latin conjugations. Colin thought about what Patrick was doing until Mr. Wheeldon, face growing alarmingly red under his thatch of white hair, smacked a ruler across Colin's hand and ordered him to stop daydreaming.

A FEW DAYS later, as Colin once again listened to Mr. Wheeldon drone on—this time about the Middle Ages—he heard hoofbeats approach through the half-open window.

It was a warm afternoon in May, and Colin longed to be outdoors. He'd thought once he was accepted to Cambridge, he'd be able to end his tutorials. However his parents had insisted on lessons all summer.

Colin's days were a numbing routine of sameness. Hours and hours of study and lessons with his tutor. Most weeks, he only left home on Sundays to attend church with his family. Although he usually daydreamed during the services, he always eagerly anticipated the end of the week and the opportunity to escape his dreary routine.

A minute later, William gave a cursory knock and swept into the study. "Ah, Mr. Wheeldon! How are you this fine day? I'm afraid my cousin will have to cut his studies short. Deepest apologies, but it's simply unavoidable." William bowed and then, with a forceful tug on Colin's arm, they were out the door before Mr. Wheeldon could reply.

Laughing as they burst out the front doors of the house, Colin breathed in the fresh air gratefully and blinked into the sun. "What's the emergency?"

"You being cooped up in that dark little room on a day such as this. School is out, my dear cousin." William had attended Eton, and Colin was thrilled to have him back. William and his parents lived only a short distance up the road, and the boys had always been close. "Come on; get your horse. The afternoon awaits."

Colin's good humor faltered. "My horse? Oh, do you think you could collect her for me? I've forgotten to tell Mr. Wheeldon something. I'll just be a moment."

William gave him a quizzical look. "What is it with you and that stable? You never want to step foot in there. Too grubby for you? No, I know what it is, my most lazy cousin. Honestly, you're spoiled quite rotten. Aunt Elizabeth and Uncle Edward did you a disservice keeping you home from school."

"Please, Will?"

"All right, since there seem to be no servants about to do your bidding, I shall. You know once we're at Cambridge, you'll have to fend for yourself!"

Colin ducked back inside the house. Since he had no message for Mr. Wheeldon and in fact wished to avoid him at all costs, he simply waited in the foyer. The upstairs maid passed, carrying a pile of curtains to be laundered. She gave him a puzzled look but scurried away before he could provide a suitable excuse for why he was skulking in the front hall.

When William whistled, Colin returned outside and swung himself onto Viola. He followed William's lead across the pasture. "Where are we going?"

"The river, of course. Where else?"

William galloped ahead confidently. They had grown up playing together, exploring the countryside around their homes. They had always been more brothers than cousins, although a stranger would not mistake them for siblings.

William was quite tall in the saddle and had golden hair. His skin loved the sun, while Colin was ever in danger of sunburns in the warmer months. Colin's own hair was a thick chestnut brown that hung over his forehead, and he was a good few inches shorter than his cousin.

As they neared the river, they slowed and let the horses saunter through a stand of trees. "I don't know how you've been able to bear that old tutor of yours. I should have gone mad long ago. Does the man ever smile?" William asked.

"Once, but I think he was passing wind."

"Well, as sheltered as you are, I suppose Aunt and Uncle were right in taking you out of classes and giving you private lessons these past years. After all, you've been accepted at Cambridge, and you never were the brightest student."

Colin didn't take offense—it was simply the truth. He knew William didn't mean any harm. "No, academics have never been my strength. I always thought I'd prefer something more physical." He thought of the countless hours in the stable with Patrick when he was younger. He'd always found far more satisfaction in mucking out a stall than in writing essays.

"Physical? *You*?" William chuckled. "You forget what a lazy sod you are. Always making me fetch your horse. What kind of physical task do you fancy you'd make a career of?"

Colin wished, not for the first time, that he could share his secret with William. But he feared if he told William of his criminal desire for Patrick and for men, he'd lose his best friend and quite possibly his life. He trusted William not to betray his confidence in every other circumstance, but feared this would be the exception. His cousin was the only person he could really talk to, but he knew he must keep William at arm's length, for both their sakes. "I really don't know. Sometimes I think being a farmer would be preferable to all those hours cooped up with textbooks."

"A *farmer*? You can't stay out in the sun for more than two hours before strongly resembling a lobster. Besides, you'd never do without all the comforts of home and servants. Academics may not be your calling, but I think you're suited to more civilized pursuits than working the land."

"Yes, I suppose you're right."

William grinned. "Naturally. Don't worry; you'll love Cambridge. We'll have a grand time. You'll make a ton of new friends so you won't have to put up with just me."

Colin smiled affectionately. "I've never needed any friend but you." William was popular with everyone, and Colin had always felt lucky to be so close with him, to have their easy camaraderie. William's friendship made him feel special.

"It's true. I am quite remarkable."

"Yet so modest."

"Incredible, isn't it?"

As they laughed, a male voice called out. "Hurry up, there! Took you long enough."

At the riverbank, five young men sunned themselves. They were some of William's chums from school, and Colin always felt woefully out of place among them. Their greetings to Colin were friendly enough as he and William joined them, but Colin was very much the outsider in the group.

Edward Lancaster had decreed that Colin was following in his footsteps at Cambridge if it was the last thing he accomplished during his time on earth. So while William had gone off and made new friends and had adventures, Colin had stayed home. His younger sister had her own tutor, but their parents were only concerned with how well she could marry. The entrance exams for Cambridge had been fearsome, but Colin had somehow passed. Barely.

He'd never been a particularly strong student. He was rather average, in fact. It was only his father's influence—and, Colin suspected, outright bribery—that had earned his place in the next Cambridge class. Although he yearned for the freedom of leaving home, the idea of more years of academics left Colin entirely cold. But just as William had asked, if Colin brought it up with anyone in his family, they wondered what he'd rather do, and he had no answer to give.

He knew there was something out there for him, but he had no notion of what it was. He was determined to find out at Cambridge. Though he wasn't enthusiastic about his studies, Colin hoped leaving home would open new doors. Perhaps he'd never live the thrilling adventures he read about in novels, but he knew there was more to life. There *had* to be.

His father had spoken fondly about the clubs he'd joined at Cambridge, of the brotherhood he'd felt with his fellow students. Although Colin was less interested in brotherhood than in developing certain *other* bonds, the idea of meeting so many new young men was greatly intriguing. He longed to go somewhere he wasn't known. Where he could be his own man for the first time. He was well and truly tired of being a boy.

"So, Lancaster. Looking forward to university?" Daniel spoke up from where he sprawled on the grass.

Colin sat and picked a wildflower, toying with the petals. "Yes, very much. You?"

"Of course. I'll undoubtedly be captain of the Oxford rowing team before long."

The other boys guffawed. "Are you planning an assassination to ease your way?" William asked.

Colin laughed loudly. He'd never cared much for Daniel. Emboldened, he joined in. "I heard you almost tipped the boat in the last race." William and the others chuckled.

Daniel's smile was smug. "Oh yes, I'm sure you're quite the expert. Trying out for the Cambridge squad, Lancaster? Perhaps your mummy and daddy should find you a private tutor so you can master the stroke."

Colin could think of no quip and simply shrugged, keeping his head down and focused on the petals he was now shredding.

A few of the others snickered, but William gave Daniel's leg a swift kick. "Watch it. It's not Colin's fault his parents are overprotective. He'll be grand at Cambridge. I know it."

Colin was warmed by William's loyalty. Fortunately, one of the others changed the subject abruptly and declared it warm enough to take a dip. Before Colin knew it, William and the others were stripping off and charging into the water, shouting. Not wanting to be teased for refusing to join in, Colin removed his clothing and followed, hurrying into the water.

Although he thought his looks were average, around William's friends, Colin felt he was quite lacking. They all seemed to be much leaner and muscled, and Colin felt rather soft in comparison, although he was slim. He wished, not for the first time, that he'd spent years rowing and playing sports so he could be fitter. Although he loved the outdoors and spent long hours walking and riding, he didn't seem to possess a natural athletic build.

The river was freezing, but with the warm sun overhead, Colin soon grew accustomed to it and paddled about happily. Treading water, he watched the others cavort. He caught flashes of nudity as they splashed and hauled each other about.

Without warning, strong arms captured Colin from behind and yanked him under the surface. He sputtered, gasping for air as he came up and heard Daniel's voice in his ear. "Come on, Lancaster. How long can you hold your breath?" Then they were back under again.

As Colin struggled, Daniel clasped him all the tighter. When he gasped for air again, Colin realized with horror that he was responding to the sensation of being held to a firm male body. With a strong backward kick to Daniel's knee, Colin broke free just as he was pulled under again. He swam out of reach as Daniel cursed. "Watch it! I was just having some fun."

"Sorry." Colin wasn't remorseful in the slightest, but the last thing he needed was a fight with Daniel, especially in his current state of arousal.

"Let's dry off in the sun." William led the way back to shore. Colin stayed in the river, willing his flesh to return to a normal state. William glanced back. "Colin?"

"Be there shortly."

William shrugged and lay out on the grass with the others. The sight of their firm bodies, skin glistening, did little to help Colin's condition, and he turned away and counted tree branches until he could venture to shore.

By the time Colin rode home, the sun was setting and he'd missed dinner. His mother would undoubtedly be displeased, especially since Mr. Wheeldon had likely reported Colin's early departure from his tutorial.

No one was about, and Colin considered going inside to ask one of the servants to return Viola to the stable. He chided himself for being a coward. Surely he could risk running into Patrick Callahan for a mere minute.

Colin led Viola to the stable as quietly as possible. All the better if he *could* avoid Patrick—or at least avoid being seen by him. Colin wouldn't mind the chance to see Patrick undetected. The thought stimulated him without fail.

As he put Viola in her pen, Colin heard an unfamiliar sound

coming from the far row of stalls. After gently latching the door on Viola's stall and giving her a treat, Colin crept around to the far row. Unlike the noises he'd heard that unforgettable day three years before, this sound was gentle and soothing.

Patrick was singing.

Stealing closer, Colin could spy Patrick with a heavily pregnant horse. The horse seemed to be in distress, and Colin realized she must be in labor.

The lullaby Patrick crooned sweetly to her was Gaelic, and Colin didn't understand the words. Then again, neither did the horse, but as Patrick stroked her flank tenderly, she nuzzled against him.

Colin watched, utterly captivated. Yes, he desired Patrick greatly, but there was something else as well. Something that drew Colin unerringly to him as a compass needle to north. He admired Patrick's confidence and skill. His physical prowess and the quiet way he could command attention. Patrick had always seemed larger than life compared to everyone else Colin knew.

Backing up slowly, Colin snuck around the corner. He took a deep breath. It was time to stop being so timid and lily-livered. If he was going to be a new person at Cambridge, he'd better start practicing now. And although his father was a close second, there was no one who intimidated him more than Patrick.

After a moment, he cleared his throat and walked with heavy footsteps toward the pregnant horse's stall. Patrick's song stopped in midverse. "Lose your way again?" As usual, sarcasm dripped heavily from Patrick's words.

"Is the horse unwell? I thought perhaps I could be of assistance." Colin's heart was lodged firmly in his throat.

Patrick's expression changed to slightly suspicious and puzzled. "She'll be fine. She's going through the worst of it now."

"Perhaps I could—"

"Go and send one of the house servants down? No need, Lord.

I'm fine on my own."

"Are you certain?"

Patrick stared for a long moment and finally shrugged. Pulse thrumming, Colin stepped into the stall. Patrick jerked his head at a bucket in the corner. "Think you can remember how to fill it?"

Colin nodded and hurried off. When he came back, feeling ridiculously proud for accomplishing his task, he asked if there was anything else.

"No. We wouldn't want you to get your hands dirty, now would we?"

"I…" Colin was as tongue-tied as ever in Patrick's presence.

"Good night, Lord." After a pause, he muttered, "Perhaps you're not completely useless."

Colin retreated quickly, returning to the house almost at a run, eager to slip away to the privacy of his chamber. When he encountered his father in the hallway, Edward gruffly asked what in the hell Colin was grinning about.

Chapter Two

WAITING ONLY A moment after knocking, Colin's mother, Elizabeth, entered his room. Colin glanced over from the window seat. He'd been watching Patrick in the meadow exercising the young colt born several days before. "Yes, Mother?"

Elizabeth was forty-two and quite beautiful, with a regal nose and posture and the same thick, chestnut brown hair as Colin. "You haven't bathed yet? Guests will be arriving within the hour."

"I was about to, if you'd leave me to my privacy."

When he wasn't studying or walking the grounds, Colin whiled away the hours sitting by his window reading novels of thrilling adventures in faraway lands. Sometimes Patrick would appear in the meadow, training the horses. Colin's book would lie forgotten on his lap as he watched Patrick at work. He seemed as if he belonged in one of the fictional tales Colin devoured. Colin could easily imagine him with sword in hand.

"Of course, dear. I had Charles press your jacket. It's hanging there." She pointed across the room, where, sure enough, his formal wear waited. "Katherine was partial to that one, if I do recall."

Colin couldn't hold back a sigh. "Yes."

"Darling, you gave up on Katherine far too easily. Tonight will be another chance for you to win her hand. You're quite a catch, you know. Off to Cambridge soon. Katherine will want to ensnare you now."

"Mother, Katherine Crawford has turned her favor elsewhere. She's moved on." So had he. Most definitely.

Elizabeth's pretty face pinched into a frown. "It's an honor that the Crawfords are attending this evening. You will be on your best behavior. I don't know what exactly you did to ruin things with Katherine, but tonight you will do your utmost to undo it."

"Yes, Mother." He would attempt no such thing, but Colin had learned years before that arguing with his parents got him nowhere. Soon he'd be at Cambridge and he would be able to make his own decisions. Soon he'd have a new life.

Mollified, Elizabeth closed the door behind her. Flopping down on his bed, Colin thought of Katherine and cringed. It wasn't until a most ill-fated outing with Katherine Crawford several months ago that Colin had admitted to himself that his interest in Patrick was far from intellectual.

Katherine was a beauty, all glossy blonde hair and moist, pink lips. For some reason Colin couldn't fathom, she had shown an interest in him at a holiday gathering down the road. The courting had begun soon thereafter, with Colin escorting Katherine on various activities. Unlike William, who railed against the inconveniences of chaperones, Colin was grateful for the matrons' presence.

He liked Katherine well enough. She was intelligent and kind and pleasing to look at. But Colin knew something was missing. Katherine didn't set his blood on fire, and he rarely thought of her when she was absent.

The absences were as long as Colin could manage while still maintaining the guise of courting. He was a perfect gentleman at all times with Katherine, which he found a simple feat. William and his school chums all needled him in private and made winking suggestions of what was actually going on between him and Katherine, and Colin let them believe what they wanted.

The Lancasters and Crawfords had both been guests at a country estate for an Easter celebration. Colin's sister, Rebecca, was delighted. On the ride over, she had chattered constantly about the beautiful Katherine and how she might one day be her sister-in-law. Colin loved his sister dearly but wished she'd find a new interest.

Colin had been fast asleep the first night at the country estate when Katherine crept into his room. Despite his protests about the impropriety, she'd insisted he dress and accompany her for a moonlight stroll. He hadn't really a choice.

It went badly.

Despite Katherine's obvious beauty and heaving bosom, Colin had remained utterly uninterested. He'd tried. Truly, he did. Under a large willow tree, Colin had kissed Katherine and caressed her soft skin under her skirt, her hand firm on his wrist, guiding him. He had been unable to get excited, and when she'd reached for him to find him flaccid, Katherine Crawford had had quite enough.

She'd stomped back to her room and avoided Colin for the remainder of the weekend. Colin could hardly meet anyone's eyes. His family had obviously required an explanation, and he'd had none.

When they returned home after a torturous journey, Colin had jumped from the carriage, eager to be away from his inquiring parents and sister, who'd demanded to know how Colin had made such a mess of things. Colin had almost barreled straight into Patrick, who had come to take the horses. At the sight of him, his lean muscles, his *maleness*, Colin had been struck with the vivid memories of what he'd witnessed in the stable that day long ago. He had to bite his tongue to stop himself from begging Patrick to take him into some dark corner and have his way with him.

That was what he wanted. He would never want the Katherine Crawfords of the world. No matter how beautiful, how rich, how ideal for a wife. Colin wanted a man. Oh, God, did he want a man.

"*Can I be of assistance?*" Patrick had affected a guileless expression, and Colin had realized he'd been staring dumbly.

Awkward and ready to crawl out of his own skin, Colin had mumbled something and hurried off. All the denials he'd repeated to himself had finally been silenced. He'd locked himself in his room, took himself in hand, and, muffling his face in a pillow as he thought of Patrick, attained the most satisfying release he'd experienced since that day at sixteen years old, hiding in the stable.

Remembering now, Colin stroked himself quickly, careful not to muss himself too much before the party. He thought of Patrick, of his Gaelic lullaby and of his grunts as he'd penetrated the man in the stable years before. As he rubbed himself with one hand, legs spread, Colin caressed his lips with his fingertips, imagining what it would be like to be kissed—*really* kissed. He didn't even know if men kissed each other, but he would like to try it.

Sometime later, Colin straightened his navy tie and vest under his dark jacket and peered into the full-length mirror in the corner of his bedroom. His large eyes were a deep brown that matched his hair, and his jaw was narrow. His nose was straight and unremarkable. Katherine had once told him that his smile turned her knees to jelly and his eyes were bottomless pools she could stare into for eternity.

Colin doubted it, somehow.

He decided he looked as presentable as he was able to and went to join the party. Naturally, the first person he saw was Katherine. Dressed to the nines in an ornate, yellow, bell-shaped gown and looking lovely, she was laughing gaily at something William had said. Her hand was placed just so on his arm, and Colin saw the flash of her eyes as she spotted him. She laughed again, even louder.

Colin felt like laughing himself. *If she only knew.* Before he could do anything, Rebecca towed him into the drawing room, her voice low and urgent, grip firm. "Honestly, I don't know what William is thinking. You mustn't pay them any mind, Colin. Are you very upset?" Her pretty face, very much like their mother's, creased with worry.

Shaking his head, Colin kissed his dear sister's cheek. "I won't give it another thought. William is welcome to her. Perhaps Father will take some solace if the family is connected to the Crawfords in the end."

Rebecca, fourteen and very dramatic, hugged him tightly. "Oh, Colin. You're ever so brave."

Biting back his mirth, Colin thanked her and pointed her toward her newly arriving friends from down the road. He made his rounds of the soiree, shaking hands and making polite conversation. Dinner was served, and Colin listened to a neighbor tell him about what a wonderful time he'd have at Cambridge. Colin hoped it would be true. The one thing dampening his excitement about finally getting away from home was that he'd also be leaving Patrick behind.

As he spooned his custard, Colin brooded. He knew it was deeply foolish, since the strange affection and desire he had for Patrick was certainly one-sided. He'd only been a child when they were friends. Even if by some miracle Patrick desired him now that he was grown, would Colin really have the nerve to lie with another man? His trousers tightened at the notion, and he was glad for the napkin across his lap.

After dinner, Colin endured the ladies' singing and gentlemen's card games. Unable to shake Patrick from his mind as the night wore on, he found himself walking to the stable, unable to stay away. He was almost there when a cry came up. A man burst out from the large wooden doors and fled across the meadow, barely visible in the darkness. In the lantern light from the stable, Patrick tumbled outside, followed by two men Colin recognized as shopkeepers in the next county. Brothers named Harris, he thought.

Colin realized he was running and skidded to a halt just as one of the brothers landed a vicious kick to Patrick's ribs. "Stop!" Colin shoved the man aside. Blood already streamed from Patrick's nose and mouth.

The man ignored Colin as if he were naught but a fly, and kicked Patrick again. "Unnatural piece of filth!"

Several other guests who heard the melee drew near. The other Harris brother called out to them. "We need the inspector. A crime's been committed here."

"What crime?" Colin demanded.

The man spit at the ground where Patrick lay beaten. "Buggery."

The world tilted on its axis, and Colin's stomach churned. He realized Patrick's breeches were loose, and that the man he'd seen fleeing must have been…

Suddenly Colin's father was there. In the lantern light, Colin could see the rage on his father's face, and it chilled him. Edward was short and stout, yet an imposing presence. He issued a terse command to the Harris brothers to follow him and bring Patrick.

Patrick was dragged around the back of the manor house, a growing number of curious guests following. Several women were told to go back to the party, and the servants watched with wide eyes as the brothers hauled Patrick through the kitchen. Inside Edward's study, a group of men gathered. Patrick was deposited on his knees in the middle of the room as Colin crowded inside with the others. They were soon joined by Colin's mother.

"What's going on?" she hissed to her husband. "There are whispers everywhere."

Edward barely spared her a glance. "This is no place for a woman. An ungodly crime has been committed. Go see to the other guests and tell them everything is fine. We don't want this getting out."

"I'm not going anywhere. Tell me what's happened!" Elizabeth's cheeks flamed.

The man who'd kicked Patrick spoke. "My wife is feeling ill, so my brother and I went to the stable to ask for our carriage to be brought round."

"Ill? Not from the food?" Elizabeth appeared horrified.

"For God's sake, woman, forget the food!" A vein in Edward's temple throbbed, and Colin feared his father might explode with rage.

"Where's the other one?" Colin glanced behind him, surprised to hear William's voice. Apparently the whispers were indeed spreading.

One of the Harris brothers answered. "Gone. I think it was the Nelsons' carriage driver. Quick bastard, we couldn't catch him. This one was still tangled up in his breeches. Caught him dead to rights."

"No need to get the courts involved. Take him out back and hang him from his bollocks," said one of the other guests.

There was a murmur of agreement, and Edward seemed to seriously be considering it. Colin's panic increased exponentially as the tension simmered. Many of those present had long been into their cups, and a reckless air swirled through the room. He looked to Patrick, who knelt silently, blood dripping down his face, his hands now bound behind his back. Colin hadn't seen who restrained him.

"Kill him," agreed one of the Harrises. To Patrick, he said, "Wouldn't you rather be put out of your misery now than rot in a jail cell knowing you're going to the gallows? We'd be doing you a favor."

The murmur of assent grew frighteningly loud. "Should have expected it from an Irishman," someone shouted.

"Hang 'im! Save the courts some time and money." The

bookkeeper from the local village reached for Patrick, attempting to haul him to his feet as other men cried their agreement.

"No!" When all eyes turned to him, Colin realized he'd spoken aloud. "*No.* You can't kill him." He thought of that day six years before, when Patrick had raced after him and plucked him from the fleeing stallion. His heart hammered as it had that day.

Edward's eyes narrowed. "Colin, the punishment for buggery is death. It's what he deserves. This man—if you can call an animal a man—is a degenerate criminal."

"Then so am I!"

Silence gripped the room in an instant, as if everyone held their breath collectively. Elizabeth went pale. "Colin, you have no idea what you're saying." She pulled his arm, urging him toward the door. "I'm sorry, everyone; he's had far too much brandy this evening. He isn't himself."

Colin yanked his arm away. "No, Mother. I know what I'm saying." He swallowed, his throat dry and thick. "I am myself." *Perhaps for the first time.*

A shocked William spoke up, his eyes wide. "Colin, this is madness!"

Edward simply stared, stunned into silence for the first time in Colin's memory. Elizabeth pulled at him again, but Colin shook free. "If you will kill this man for his crime, then you'll have to kill me too. Shall you take me outside and string me up?"

"What in God's name are you doing?" Patrick spoke for the first time, and all eyes turned to where he knelt. He stared at Colin with dazed astonishment.

The sound of Patrick's voice seemed to spur Edward out of his daze. Edward turned a murderous gaze on Patrick. "If you've laid a finger on my son, I swear—"

"I'd sooner bed a horse," Patrick sneered.

"And probably has!" a voice called out.

Colin felt a ridiculous stab of pain at Patrick's words.

Patrick went on. "Sir, your son is clearly not in his right mind."

William's father, John, a lawyer, spoke next. He was tall and distinguished, the opposite of his brother, Edward. He seemed to be the only calm person left in the room. "Colin, are you saying you've committed acts of buggery?"

"Yes." Even if it wasn't true, Colin couldn't let them kill Patrick. At least not tonight, not if he could help it.

Elizabeth shrieked and collapsed into a chair. "Oh, my son. What have you done? It can't be true!"

"I'm sorry, Mother. They'll have to kill us both."

"Don't listen to him! For God's sake!" Patrick tried to stand but was shoved back down by Edward, whose face flamed with rage.

John spoke up. "No one's killing anyone." He turned to the Harris brothers. "Did you witness the act?"

One of them laughed tersely. "Didn't have to. They heard us coming, and the other one was off and running. But we saw and heard enough to know what was going on."

John pondered this, and everyone waited. He seemed to have quietly taken control of the proceedings, for which Colin was grateful. He hoped Patrick wouldn't be harmed any further for the moment.

"No concrete evidence. None in regards to Colin either," John said after a lengthy pause.

"Because it's *not true*!" Elizabeth cried.

John ignored her and turned to Edward. "I have some friends in the magistrate's office who should be able to help. I'll go speak to George Crawford and get him on our side. But too many people have heard Colin's confession. Something must be done."

Edward nodded grimly, not looking at Colin. He pointed to Patrick. "We'll keep this one locked in the pantry for the night. Colin will be in his room with a guard placed outside. William, take him upstairs."

The shock of his actions slowly settling in, Colin didn't resist as William led him away. They opened the door to the study to find the hallway crowded with party guests. Katherine was among them, her delicate face transformed into a hard mask. "Fiend!" She dashed down the hall, weeping.

Accusing eyes glared from all sides, and William led Colin to the servants' back stairway, sparing him the spectacle of being marched up the grand staircase. In his room, Colin tried to speak. "Will, I…"

William raised a hand. "Don't." He shook his head sadly, his expression deeply wounded. "I don't understand. I've always thought of you as a dear friend. A brother. Now I feel I've never known you at all." He turned his back, closing the door behind him. A moment later, Colin heard the key turn in the lock, and his life as he knew it was over.

Chapter Three

COLIN WASN'T SURE what woke him. He blinked at the morning light streaming through the windows and wondered why he was still dressed, laying atop his blankets—

He remembered the events of the previous night with a sickening churn in the pit of his stomach. *What had he done*? He closed his eyes, replaying it all in his mind. He'd paced around his room for hours until finally falling asleep sometime before dawn.

Taking a deep breath, Colin blew it out slowly. He had spoken aloud a truth he'd taken years to accept. Even if he'd never actually performed the acts himself, he'd sinned in his heart and mind. Given half the chance, he'd eagerly lie with another man.

Colin heard the twist of metal, and William appeared in the doorway. He looked as exhausted as Colin felt. His suit was rumpled, and he didn't appear to have slept. Colin swung his legs over the side of the bed and sat, waiting. William perched stiffly beside him.

"You've never…*been* with a man." It was a statement, not a question. William knew Colin too well to believe his bold proclamations.

Colin shook his head.

"But you wish to."

Holding his breath, Colin nodded. After a long moment of silence dragged on, Colin dared to look at his cousin. To his utter horror, William's eyes glistened with tears. "Will—"

"You can't mean it. I don't understand how it's possible. You're my best friend. I would have known. I *should* have known." William wiped his eyes, to no avail. "Why didn't you tell me?"

"I wanted to! Oh, I wanted to. But how could I? What would you have said?"

William grasped Colin's shoulder, his words earnest. "You're confused. We can work this out. You don't need to condemn yourself. Take back what you said last night. Tell them it was a lie. A foolish lie!"

Colin shook his head sadly. "No, Will. I know what I feel. It took me years to understand it. To accept it. But I know you can't."

Bolting up, William paced. "Of course not! It's *wrong*, Colin. It's a crime. A sin. You have a sickness."

"It doesn't feel that way to me. It feels right. Natural." It was fantastical to actually express these thoughts out loud.

"But what kind of life do you want? A life of depravity? Of misery?"

Colin exhaled slowly. It was a fine question. "I don't know. Not this." Colin gestured about him. "I've never been happy. Never fit in. I don't know what kind of life is possible for me now, but I know I can't go back. For better or worse, that life is over."

"Don't say that, Colin." William seemed stricken.

"At least now I don't have to carry this secret. There's freedom in that, Will. A strange sort of happiness."

William took that in for a few moments. He shook his head as if defeated. "We had such plans. I thought we'd do everything together. Go to Cambridge. Find wives eventually, have families. But now…"

"You'll make a good husband, Will. A good father. I hope one day I can be your friend again. Know your family, even." The thought of not having William in his life was sorrowful. Colin swallowed thickly over the lump in his throat.

William paled. "They haven't told you."

A new fear flared to life, and Colin's voice was hoarse. "Told me?"

"The prisons. They're already overcrowded. There's simply no room."

Panic thrummed in Colin's veins. "To the gallows, then?"

"No, no. To Australia."

"The penal colony?" Colin was stunned. This outcome hadn't occurred to him in all his hours of pacing and worrying. He didn't know what to think. *Australia.* The word itself sounded foreign and strange.

"There's a ship sailing two days hence. You're leaving for port later today, arriving tomorrow."

"Today? So soon. Patrick too?" Colin felt as if he'd wake at any moment and this would all be but a fearsome dream.

"Yes."

Colin was flooded with relief. At least he'd saved Patrick's life. That was something he could never regret. "*Australia.* I never imagined I'd actually leave England."

"It's the other side of the world."

"Yes, I suppose it is." Colin realized he would never meet William's children. Emotion choked his voice. "I shall miss you." His eyes welled. "So very much. What will I do without you?"

William wiped his own tears and yanked Colin to his feet, hands firm on his shoulders. "You shall be brave. You'll get through it."

"I'm so frightened, Will." A sob racked Colin, and he threw himself in his cousin's arms. For a moment, William tensed, but then he held Colin close.

When they separated, William straightened his jacket and took long breaths. "I won't see you again before you leave."

Colin had never known grief so intense. He struggled to maintain his composure.

"Promise you'll write."

Colin blinked in surprise, sniffling. "You'd accept my letters?"

William smiled sadly. "Always, Colin. Always."

With that, he was gone. Colin curled up on his bed, still in the previous night's finery, and cried until there was nothing left.

A FEW HOURS later, Colin's mother strode into his room. He'd changed into what he considered sensible clothing for sailing on a convict ship—sturdy trousers and a cotton shirt. Elizabeth stood there, eyes puffy, face drawn. When Colin started to speak, she held up her hand.

"The magistrate will be here shortly. They've worked it all out. You will plead guilty, and he will accept your plea."

"Guilty to what?"

Elizabeth struggled to utter the words. "Attempted buggery." She appeared nauseated. "Be thankful this lesser charge doesn't carry the death sentence. If there were hard proof, you'd both end up hanging."

"Instead it's off to Australia." Colin was still in a state of shock. The very notion that he would soon be on a convict ship was outlandish.

Elizabeth shuddered and suppressed a sob. Colin opened his arms and stepped toward her. "Mother—"

"No!" She stumbled back, her sobs becoming shrieks. "Don't touch me! You sicken me!"

Colin retreated, crossing his arms over his stomach, trying very hard to keep his composure. "I'm sorry."

"I can't even bear to look at you! You father wouldn't come up here with me." She wailed. "What have we done to deserve this? How could this happen? This *perversion*! In *our* son. Under *our* roof! We gave you everything, and you spit it back in our faces!"

"I never meant to hurt you."

Elizabeth laughed, a brittle sound. "As if you thought of us at all. I don't want to know with whom you've committed these unnatural acts. I shudder to think it was that Irish piece of filth. Tell me; did he lead you down this path to damnation?"

Unbidden, Colin's mind flickered back to that rainy afternoon in the stable. Patrick had only unknowingly shown Colin his true desires. "No, Mother."

She narrowed her gaze, and for the first time, Colin felt unnervingly that his mother truly could see into his soul. "I don't believe you. You must care for him. To have spoken as you did last night." Fresh tears spilled onto her cheeks. "You care more for *him* than your own family! Our reputation! Oh, I hope it was worth it, Colin." She turned and fled, locking the door emphatically behind her.

Colin sank down on his window seat. The glass was cool against his forehead, and he steadied his breathing. There would be no more watching for William coming down the drive. No more spying Patrick and the horses in the meadow.

He'd been fascinated and frightened by Patrick, and compelled by him in a way he couldn't explain. When he'd thought Patrick might die, Colin had experienced an agony and panic he hadn't thought possible. He thought of his mother's accusations. *Was it worth it?*

Now that Pandora's box was opened, Colin felt a strange relief. No more courting young women he had no interest in. No more textbooks and studies he didn't care about. No more hiding. For better or worse, the truth was out.

AS THE DAY progressed, the "worse" side of the equation weighed heavily on the scale. William's father escorted Colin down to Edward's study, where the magistrate waited. Colin's father was nowhere to be seen. The magistrate, a small and stern-faced man, said the proceedings were highly unusual and that Colin should be extremely grateful. He pointed to the blank spot where Colin was to sign.

The ink had barely dried when Colin heard a vehicle rumble up the drive. Uncle John led him outside, past the servants, who all tried without success to appear busy. At the sight of Patrick standing at the bottom of the front steps, hands still bound behind him, Colin's heart leaped. He was relieved Patrick appeared none the worse for wear since he'd seen him last, although bruises darkened his face.

A covered prison wagon with bars on the small windows rumbled to a stop. Colin swallowed, his throat suddenly dry. *You're a criminal now.*

He heard a distressed sound behind him and turned just in time to catch Rebecca as she hurled herself into his arms. She hugged Colin fiercely, and his heart constricted. Rebecca was a good sister, and he would miss her. "It's not a life sentence. You'll be back before we know it, won't you?" She sniffed loudly.

Colin glanced at the stone faces of his parents on the steps, his father finally having appeared. Colin knew he would never be welcomed in England again. He kissed Rebecca's sodden cheek. "We shall see. Remember that I love you. Be a good girl for Mother and Father."

Rebecca ran back into the house, the sound of her sobs trailing behind her. Colin waited for his parents to step forward, but they remained frozen. Finally he nodded at them and turned away, concentrating on breathing in and out. The magistrate and the prison guard went over the papers, and before Colin knew it, he and Patrick were herded into the back of the small transport. Patrick was unbound, and they were each shackled with iron to the side of the wagon.

There appeared to be no rush, and the guard and magistrate continued their conversation outside. Colin wished they'd just get on with it.

"I don't understand you." Patrick's voice was loud in the confines of the wagon. They each sat on a wooden bench on either side, knees almost touching.

Colin had no idea how to respond. "I…"

"I know you're lying."

"How?"

"I just do. You haven't been running around getting buggered any more than the king has."

Colin didn't argue this fact. "I wanted to help you."

"You haven't had any use for me for years. So why now?"

"I owe you. You rescued me."

Patrick's expression was unreadable. "The stallion? When you were a boy?"

Colin nodded.

"Turns out you're still as foolish as you were that day. Well, don't go thinking *I* owe you a damn thing, Lord Lancaster. I didn't ask for your help."

"I saved your life." Colin had hoped for a sliver of gratitude. Or even just a lack of hostility.

"So I could get shipped off to some hellish corner of the world? I've lost everything I've worked for. I'd sooner be hung, quick and easy."

Colin exhaled in frustration. "Well, don't worry. I'm sure you can find a way to do yourself in. Jumping from the ship midocean would likely be highly effective."

Patrick stared at him for a moment and then barked out a surprising laugh. "All right. I'm not going to jump, and I suppose Australia is better than the gallows. Just don't go thinking we're friends. We're not. We're strangers, and it's going to stay that way.

You'll go your way, and I'll go mine."

"Understood." Perhaps he'd be able to change Patrick's mind about him during the long voyage. Make him understand that Colin wasn't the foolish boy Patrick thought he was.

"Good." Patrick leaned back and shut his eyes.

"That man. The carriage driver."

Patrick didn't open his eyes. "What about him?"

"Did you…know him well?"

"Don't even know the quick bastard's name. He was hardly worth the trouble, but that's life for you."

Colin tried to imagine being intimate with a complete stranger and failed miserably. Uncle John appeared at the wagon door. He reached in, and for a moment, he covered Colin's hand with his own. "Good luck, Colin. I hope you can make something of your life in the end." He stepped back, and the door clanged shut. With a jolt, they were off. Patrick kept his eyes shut, appearing unaffected by the fact that they were being taken away as criminals.

Colin peered out one of the barred windows for a last glance of his home and parents. His mother's shoulders shook as she watched him being taken away. His father had already turned, and he disappeared into the house a moment later. Then the wagon drove around the curve in the drive, and Colin's home disappeared.

Chapter Four

AS THE PRISON wagon finally rumbled into Portsmouth, Colin was filled with relief. The journey had been long and painful. While the driver and guard had taken breaks for sleep and enjoyed meals along the way in taverns, Colin and Patrick had been left in the stuffy heat of the padlocked wagon. They'd only been allowed out to urinate every so often.

Colin yearned to stretch his limbs and be unshackled. Unsurprisingly, Patrick had said little, and Colin had had naught else to do but worry endlessly about what would happen next. The fact that he was now a convicted criminal with nothing more than the clothes on his back seemed absurd. Colin had never faced the unknown as he did now.

He and Patrick had both slept fitfully, but now they were awake and on edge as they neared their destination. The Portsmouth dockyard was a noisy, gritty place. Colin turned as best he could to get a look through the bars on the tiny window. He caught a whiff of sea air and felt desperate to be out of the oppressive confines of the wagon.

When they finally came to a halt, it seemed the guard was in no hurry whatsoever to free them. The minutes ticked by. Both Patrick and Colin bore a sheen of sweat, and Colin wondered when he'd actually bathe again. He suspected it would not be soon.

"Bloody hell." Patrick rattled his shackled wrist. "Let us out of here!"

They were ignored, and time crawled by until Colin was sure it had to have been more than an hour since they'd arrived. His throat was parched, and the air was so thick he felt as though it was pressing against him.

Just when he thought he couldn't take another moment before going mad, the back door creaked open. The guard peered in dispassionately. Before Colin could stop himself, he exclaimed, "It's about time!"

The guard regarded him evenly for a moment before laughing heartily. "Better get used to it, lad! You ain't gonna be resting in the lap of luxury no longer." He sneered. "You'll be lucky if you even make it down there alive."

Another guard joined him and shared in the merriment at Colin's expense. "You's a proper gentleman, eh? Good luck to ya!" But at least Colin and Patrick were unshackled and taken out of the wagon. Colin's legs wobbled as he stepped down, the muscles tense and cramped.

Although the air carried a myriad of scents, some decidedly unpleasant, Colin breathed it deeply as they were shunted along toward a large ship. The name read *LADY HAREWOOD*, which Colin thought an incongruously pretty name considering the ship's function. At the gang-board, a group of prisoners said goodbye to their families. A woman wailed and children wept. Colin thought of his parents and turned away from the scene.

The ship was a frigate with three masts. Men crowded the main deck. Colin and Patrick were led aboard, where the convicts waited under the watchful gaze of armed guards. Another group of men surged on behind them, and before Colin knew it, he and Patrick were separated.

As the day dragged on and they waited endlessly, the prisoners were given rations of water and stale rolls of bread. Colin devoured his quickly and was still starving.

"What you in for?" A man with missing teeth elbowed Colin.

"Uh, I…" Colin was at a loss.

"They got me for pickpocketing. Like those fancy folks in London can't spare a bit of change, eh?" He laughed, although it was more of a wheeze.

"Same. Pickpocketing."

"We should 'ave been quicker!"

Colin laughed along, although he felt no mirth. "Yes. Quite."

The man's expression changed. "Where you from, boy? Sound pretty highborn for a pocketer. You sure that's what you in for?"

Colin's nod was vigorous. "Uh huh." He vowed to say as little as possible on the voyage lest the others pick up on his upper-class accent.

When the captain stood on the upper deck to address them sometime later, Colin was relieved. He just wanted to get on with it already. The captain was a pockmarked, middle-aged man with a paunch and his dark hair tied back at his neck. His expression was stern, and his tone brooked no argument.

After some shouts from the guards, the prisoners fell silent and the captain spoke. "I'm Captain Stonehouse. This vessel is the *Lady Harewood*. You will treat her with respect. Every last one of you." He paused for effect before going on.

"One hundred and ninety-nine souls will leave England on this ship. God willing, we will all reach Sydney in one hundred and twenty-four days. Give or take. Of the one hundred and ninety-nine, some are settlers. Some are crew. Most of you are the dregs of society. You will treat your betters and each other with respect, or you will pay the consequences.

"Believe me when I tell you that the consequences will be severe. We don't spare the lash on this vessel."

A murmur rippled through the prisoners, and one of the guards stepped forward menacingly.

"However, these are enlightened times. We have with us Reverend Sewell, who is a forward thinker in regard to prisoners' needs." The captain indicated a young, black-clad, red-haired man to his right. The reverend nodded, and the captain continued. "You will receive fair rations and the chance to exercise above decks during the day. Be grateful. Remember that these privileges can and will be taken from you if deemed necessary.

"Your quarters on this ship have recently been renovated. You will all be given bunk space instead of the floor. Again, be grateful. You will not be kept in irons unless it's deemed necessary." He turned and indicated another man. "Our doctor is Dr. Fairfowl." A thin, bespectacled man beside the reverend stood up straighter. "Pray you will not need his attention.

"We are leaving shortly. Take a long, last look at England, for you shall surely never step on its hallowed ground again."

With that, the captain took his leave. Families and sweethearts lined the shore, and prisoners shouted final farewells. When the boat was free of its moorings, Colin did take a good look as Portsmouth receded. No one gestured to him from the shore, but he found himself waving anyway.

NIGHT FELL AS they left the English Channel, and the prisoners were herded to their quarters. As they descended into the belly of the ship, the air grew stale and humid. The lowest deck on the ship had been divided into two barred sections, with the guards' station in the center. The iron doors on either side led to the barracks.

The men filed in and were given their uniforms. One of the guards shouted instructions. "Take your slops and put 'em on. Toss your old clothes in the sack." When Colin's turn came, he quickly stripped off and stepped into too-big canvas trousers. He buttoned the striped cotton shirt quickly and carried the gray wool jacket over his arm. All the items were marked with the broad arrow identifying government property.

As the prisoners moved through, a guard ticked names off his list and assigned them their beds. The guard, a large man with sloping shoulders and a heavy brow, sized him up. "Name."

"Lancaster. Colin." Colin was relieved his voice didn't squeak. Sweat dripped down his spine, and his heart raced. He could see into the barracks, and along with narrow single bunks lining the hull, there was a bank down the center of the ship which would sleep men side by side on the upper and lower levels. Colin prayed he'd get an outside berth.

The guard, called Ford according to the name stitched on his jacket, consulted his list. "Lancaster." His gaze flicked over the page, and Colin knew from Ford's expression that his crime was listed there. Ford lifted his heavy brow. "Perhaps you'd enjoy a middle bunk. They sleep four across."

Colin stammered as his heart plummeted. "I… No… Please, sir."

Ford seemed to relent with a sly chuckle. "Lancaster. Bunk number eighty-five. Top."

Another guard handed Colin a rough blanket and gave him a shove toward the barracks on the stern end. Colin made his way down the narrow aisle until he found his bunk. To his enormous relief, the bunk was a single on the hull side. No one was below him yet, so Colin stepped on the lower bunk to boost himself up. The bed, if one could call it that, was slender and constructed of coarse wood. There was no mattress or pillow.

Sitting on his berth, Colin peered around the dim hold, which was lit by lanterns hung on the wall at intervals. He searched among the men for Patrick but couldn't see him. Colin hoped he wasn't on the other side of the ship.

Sitting there on his hard new bed, he'd never felt so alone in all his years. He thought of his family and especially of William, and the sense of terrible loss gnawed at him. Although they hadn't had their dinner ration yet, Colin lay down and pillowed his head on his arm. Despite the heat and utter lack of ventilation, he pulled the blanket up over him and closed his eyes with determination, escaping the only way he could.

COLIN WOKE WITH a start sometime later as the ship rocked alarmingly. In the darkness around him, Colin could hear a mix of prayers and curses as they rocked on the rough sea. The stench of vomit soon filled the dank air, and Colin feared he'd be ill himself. He breathed through his nose and tried to return to the haven of sleep, but it was no use.

He had no idea what time it was, and the only faint light shone distantly from the guards' station. He wondered where Patrick was. Although he knew Patrick had said they weren't friends, he couldn't help but hope that would change.

After what seemed like an eternity, Colin fell back into a fitful sleep. When morning came, he discovered some of the prisoners had been assigned the role of leader of a group. The groups were taken to the main deck in turn to wash themselves in metal basins. Once a week, they would be allowed to shave. Colin breathed the morning sea air deeply, quite relieved to be outside and seeing the sun, which had just risen.

He longed for the privacy of his old bedroom at home, as it was clear that there would be none on the *Lady Harewood*. Once they were washed, they filed back down to the prison deck, where they were given their breakfast. Colin soon discovered all meals were essentially the same: stale bread, some rice, and salt pork or salt beef—a cut of meat from the belly of the beast cured in salt and soaked in water before being cooked. It was a staple of most ships' cuisine since it lasted a very long time before spoiling.

After breakfast and cleaning of utensils and the prison deck itself, the men were all allowed onto the main deck. As Reverend Sewell gave a morning sermon, Colin glanced around, looking for Patrick. He found him about twenty men away. At one point, Patrick looked over and met Colin's gaze for a long moment before turning.

Exercise and general activity was permitted once the reverend was finished. Colin kept to himself, walking around the ship's perimeter. The settlers were separated from the convicts on a smaller upper deck. Colin watched them and wondered who they were and why they'd choose to leave England behind. He wished he had more to look forward to in Australia besides years in prison.

They were herded back to the barracks for lunch, and then allowed out again for a portion of the afternoon. There was a rustic water closet at each end of the ship, and although it emptied into the sea, the stench could be overwhelming. He didn't look forward to being on cleaning duty.

Then it was back down for supper, followed by prayers and being confined to their beds. While the others conversed, Colin tried his best to be inconspicuous. He didn't want to garner any unnecessary attention. The lights went out at eight o'clock, and any men caught speaking or moving about were punished.

Each day was a repeat of the previous with the exception of Sunday, when Reverend Sewell pontificated even longer than usual on society's ills and God's salvation. He read long, meandering passages from the Bible, and at times Colin had to struggle to stay awake.

Colin had discovered Patrick's berth was on the same end of the ship, but on the other side of the hull and closer to the rear. One afternoon on the main deck, Colin sought him out. Patrick was playing cards with a group of other Irishmen. They'd seemed to gravitate toward each other as birds of a feather would, and Colin envied their camaraderie. He felt woefully out of place among the prisoners, and he certainly wasn't allowed to socialize with the settlers.

He sat nearby and watched Patrick and the others play. Patrick acknowledged him with a raised eyebrow but said nothing. He wondered if the others knew of Patrick's crime. Or perhaps they shared the same proclivities. As Patrick laughed with one of them over a private joke, jealousy prickled Colin. He wanted Patrick to laugh easily with him as he once had when Colin was a boy.

The thought that they would likely be separated and sent to different prisons upon arrival was something Colin did his utmost not to dwell on, with little success. There was naught he could do to prevent it, but it plagued him.

After a spell, he moved on, not wanting to garner the attention of Patrick's new friends. He had to sweep the prison deck after dinner, and he threw himself into the work with relish. The rough conditions wouldn't kill him, but the boredom might.

TWO WEEKS AFTER leaving England, they encountered a storm and the ship rocked on the waves frighteningly. Colin worried he might tumble from his tiny berth. He gripped the side of the bunk and told himself that everything would be fine, that the rolling was surely normal. His stomach lurched in concert with the ship, and sounds of retching once again echoed in the musty air. After a while, the seas calmed somewhat and Colin gratefully drifted to sleep.

With a sickening jolt, he was suddenly falling. As Colin woke, a hand clamped over his mouth, and he realized he was being pulled from his bunk. There was a crack of pain in his knees as he hit the floor; then rough hands shoved him face down over the side of the lower bunk. Fetid breath puffed by his ear. "Right, now. Jus' be a good boy and don't put up a fight. It ain't gonna hurt. *Much.*"

Instinctively Colin kicked backward and struggled. His heart hammered in his chest, and as he cried out, the sound was muffled by the meaty palm plastered over his mouth. He squirmed desperately in the darkness, to no avail. Snores drifted on the musty air, and though Colin kicked and tried to wake someone—anyone—the other prisoners seemed dead to the world.

As Colin's trousers were yanked down, he cried out again, but his jaw was painfully immobilized. Another man chuckled. "We heard what you're in for. Don't fret; you'll like it."

It felt as if there were hands everywhere, pinning him down, slithering over his bared flesh. The side of the bunk dug painfully into his stomach, and Colin was feverish with fear, his mind screaming as he tried to fight.

There was a loud *thump*, followed by several grunts and a commotion around him. Suddenly Colin could breathe freely again, and he opened his mouth, gasping for air. The hands were gone. He spun around, collapsing onto the floor.

"This one's mine." Patrick miraculously loomed overhead, holding one man by the throat as he glared at the other two sprawled on the floor. His tone brooked no argument. "Glance at him sideways, let alone touch him again, and it'll be the last thing you mongrels do."

Colin wasn't sure how Patrick had fought off the attackers, but as quickly as they'd materialized, they skulked back into the night. Then Patrick was kneeling before him. It was difficult to see his face clearly in the darkness, but he seemed anxious. Colin laughed, a hysterical sound. He must have sustained a head injury. He was clearly seeing things.

"Come on." With surprising gentleness, Patrick lifted Colin to his feet. Colin's canvas trousers had pooled around his ankles, and

Patrick reached down and pulled them up, redoing the fastenings as Colin swayed.

Patrick guided him along the narrow aisle, past sleeping men, to his own bottom bunk on the far side. He urged Colin down and followed. Colin lay on his side, facing the wall, with Patrick behind him. Between him and the rest of the prisoners.

Despite the oppressive heat, Colin shivered. Patrick rested his hand lightly on Colin's upper arm. "Did they hurt you? Did they…"

Colin shuddered as he thought of their greasy hands on his skin, and his pulse still raced. He'd never longed to bathe more in his entire life. "They were going to…to…" He found himself unable to say the words.

"Shh, it's all right now." Patrick stroked Colin's hair soothingly. "Go to sleep."

Patrick's presence on the narrow bunk was overwhelming, his large body pressed against Colin's in the tiny space. Yet Colin felt safer than he had since he'd boarded the *Lady Harewood*, and slowly he steadied himself. Listening to Patrick's breathing, he finally let it lull him into dreams.

LIGHTS BURNED WHEN Colin jerked awake. He took a shuddering breath and shook off the vestiges of a nightmare of suffocation and hands, hands, hands. His heart raced.

"It was just a dream." Patrick sat on the edge of the bunk and glanced at Colin over his shoulder.

Colin pushed himself up, wincing as pain flared in his ribs. "Much damage?"

Although everything felt extremely tender, Colin shook his head. "I'm fine." He told himself sternly to stop wishing his mother would appear to take him in her arms and make everything better. She hadn't done so since he was a small child anyway. "You must think me very pitiful."

"Why's that?"

"I couldn't stop them. I tried, but—"

"There were three of them and one of you. Not odds many men could overcome. You've nothing to be ashamed of."

Colin knew he was right, but couldn't help but feel weak and fearful. After gingerly shifting to sit beside Patrick on the side of the bunk, Colin noticed the fresh blood on the knuckles of Patrick's right hand. He reached out tentatively and touched the wounds. Patrick moved his hand out of reach.

"You're taking the bunk over mine. The thief up there decided to relocate to the other side of the hold."

A flush of pleasure and pride soothed Colin. *Patrick fought for me.* He'd forced Colin's way into the bunk above, and the night before, he'd... A thought occurred to Colin, rather belatedly. "How did you know?"

"Know?"

"That they were...that I was in need of assistance last night."

Shrugging, Patrick looked away. "You're lucky, Lord. I had to take a piss and heard the fuss."

"From all the way over here?"

Abruptly, Patrick stood. "Just keep out of my way and out of trouble. You can't rely on me. Understand?"

Colin opened his mouth to reply, but Patrick was already striding away.

Chapter Five

IN THE DAYS that followed, Colin tried to go on as if nothing had happened. Yet his skin felt as if it crawled, and although he scoured himself raw when he bathed, he wished he could stay in the steel basin all day, scrubbing.

He hadn't gotten a good look at his attackers and was even more wary of the other prisoners than he had been before. He found himself sleeping more in the daytime, outside on the deck. He closed his eyes whenever he had the chance and imagined he was anywhere else.

Colin hated being so weak. Yet he felt unaccountably ashamed for what had happened. He should have been more alert, more ready to defend himself. He should have been able to fight them off. Should have been stronger. Faster. Better.

The days ticked by slowly, the monotony setting in. Colin slept fitfully at night, afraid to be off guard if he slumbered too deeply. He lay awake, listening to the snores and rustles around him, constantly wary. Patrick's presence below him was a comfort, but Colin still feared the night.

One morning after prayers, Reverend Sewell approached Colin where he sat on the wooden deck in the shade, eyes closed.

"Colin, isn't it?"

Colin opened his eyes and nodded cautiously. He'd never had much interest in the church aside from the opportunity to go into town every week. He hadn't taken to the sermons the way his parents had. Perhaps because he knew deep down he was a sinner—or worse—in the church's eyes.

The reverend took a seat beside him. He was a young man, likely fresh from the seminary. Ginger freckles dotted his pale skin, and Colin mused they would both have to battle the sun in Australia. "How are you adjusting? You look quite tired."

Colin hadn't seen his reflection since leaving his bedroom at home. "Do I?" He wondered what he would see the next time he had occasion to look in a mirror. He remembered his manners and added, "Thank you for asking."

"You're well-bred. This must be a difficult transition."

Colin had to laugh. "Yes, you could say that."

"You certainly stand out among the murderers and rapists. Even the petty thieves."

"Yes, I must. A weakling compared to them."

The reverend frowned. "Not at all. You just don't have a lifetime of experience dealing with these harsh situations as they do. I must confess, I'm finding it a challenge to make any progress with the inmates on the whole. I'm quite out of my element as well."

Colin was surprised to be taken into the reverend's confidence and found he was pleased. "Why are you here? Going to the other side of the world? Couldn't you have had a parish somewhere in England?"

"Yes, I could have. But I felt the need would be greater here among the convicts and in the new society in Australia. My life can have greater meaning in the colony. I can serve God better."

"An admirable goal."

Sewell smiled. "I like to think so."

Colin found himself smiling too, and it was a welcome change. "I wish I were going to Australia to find greater purpose."

"Perhaps you are. God has a plan, you know. If you let go of the past, you can embrace the future. Become a new person."

"Perhaps." Colin wasn't sure what kind of person he'd become in prison.

Sewell glanced at his timepiece. "I'm afraid I must go and see to the children's schooling. I've tried to persuade the captain into letting me hold classes for the prisoners, but he already chafes against the enlightened conditions you're enjoying. Getting to come up for air at all is an improvement."

"I shudder to imagine how it was before."

"Yes, I've heard disturbing tales from the crew. Quite disturbing." Sewell got to his feet. "I've enjoyed our conversation, Colin. Do get some sleep, and don't be so hard on yourself. I hope we can speak again."

Colin called after him as the reverend walked away. "Thank you."

Sewell acknowledged him with a nod. Colin felt refreshed after their discussion. Instead of closing his eyes and escaping to an imaginary world, he watched the reverend on the upper deck with the closely guarded children. He'd heard that some of the guards were settlers themselves and had brought their families.

Colin envied them. At least they were going into the unknown together. At the thought, he glanced about for Patrick and blinked in surprise to find Patrick watching him across the deck. Patrick turned sharply and spoke to one of the Irishmen, but Colin smiled to himself. Perhaps he was having an effect on Patrick after all.

That night he slept soundly, determined not to be ruled by his fear. Yet the nightmares came once more, hands gripping him, smothering him. He gasped awake to find a figure standing by the bunk. He shied away, pressing himself against the hull.

"'Tis only me." Patrick's tone was soothing, and Colin unclenched his muscles.

"I'm sorry to wake you." Colin's voice was little more than a croak, and his heart hammered. He wondered if he'd ever have a decent night's rest again.

"Come on." Patrick gave him a gentle tug, and Colin gratefully slid off the bunk. Patrick urged him onto his own berth, and Colin lay on his side toward the hull, with Patrick large and reassuring behind him, just as they had the night of the attack. "Now sleep," Patrick commanded.

Amazingly, Colin did. He woke in the darkness some hours later, unsure of the time but feeling that morning would soon be upon them. The faint light from the guards' station provided the only light. Colin stretched his limbs as best he could without disturbing Patrick.

He'd slept deeply, and as he shifted, he realized the day must indeed be fast approaching as his morning stiffness made itself known for the first time since boarding the ship. *Well rested indeed*. He hadn't touched himself in weeks, and he rubbed his cock with the heel of his hand through his trousers.

Patrick cleared his throat, and Colin froze. "Good morning." Patrick's tone was light.

Colin yanked his hand away as if his trousers were alight, and his face flamed. Patrick rolled Colin onto his back with gentle pressure on his shoulder. In the dimness, Colin could just make out Patrick's puzzlement. "I was only teasing." He spoke quietly, as the men around them hadn't stirred. "Don't feel badly."

"But I shouldn't…"

"What?"

"You know."

"Feel pleasure? Don't be embarrassed by it. There's precious little in life to enjoy as it is."

"It's just…" Colin took a deep breath. "I spent years feeling guilty. And then those men, they made me feel so…" He struggled to put it into words. "Humiliated."

"Listen to me. You've nothing to be ashamed of. *Nothing*. It's a natural thing."

Colin's breath hitched as Patrick reached down and stroked

him lightly through the rough material. In the still of the dawn, curled together on the tiny bunk, it was as if they were in their own world. Warm pleasure unfurled as Patrick touched him. Patrick stilled his hand, and peered at Colin intently. "Tell me if you want to stop."

It was quite possibly the very furthest thing from Colin's mind. "Please go on."

He'd dreamed of being touched by Patrick so many times that he wasn't sure if this was a fantasy or not. His body tingled, and his hips lifted of their own accord so Patrick could peel down Colin's pants and drawers, freeing his cock and bollocks.

Squeezing farther down on the bunk, Patrick dipped his head. Colin wondered what he was doing just before Patrick's lips met the head of Colin's cock. He gasped in astonishment and awe at the heady feeling as Patrick caressed him lightly with his tongue. Colin had heard bawdy tales from William and his school chums about the acts wanton ladies performed, but he'd never quite believed them.

Patrick's mouth and hands were infinitely gentle, and he took Colin deeper, stroking and sucking him. The tight, wet sensation was incredible. Colin's entire body felt lighter than air, and he imagined he would have floated right up into the bottom of his bunk if not for Patrick's weight.

The sparks of pleasure curled outward from his cock like tendrils. He breathed shallowly through his parted lips, careful to stay quiet, wishing he could shout his joy to the heavens.

As Patrick pleasured him with his mouth, sweet pressure built in Colin's loins. Patrick seemed to know just where to touch, and with the perfect amount of pressure from his lips and tongue. The tension finally exploded in a wave that swept Colin's body and left him trembling. He sucked in a deep breath as he returned to earth. He'd spilled in Patrick's mouth, but Patrick didn't seem to mind in the least, and he cleaned Colin's cock with lazy swipes of his tongue, sending tremors all the way to Colin's toes.

Light flared, and one of the guards boomed, "Wake up!" The guards would now be out to light lanterns throughout the hold. Patrick tossed Colin the discarded blanket from the foot of the bed and disappeared up onto Colin's bunk in the blink of an eye. If one of the guards caught them sharing a single berth, there would be serious consequences.

It was Ford who ambled down their side of the hold. He paused by their bunk, and Colin's heart thumped as Ford leaned down. "Weren't you on the other side when we left England?"

Colin tried to formulate an excuse, but no words would come. To his complete shock, Ford's mouth twitched into a smile after a moment. Then he was gone, continuing on his rounds. Colin breathed a sigh of relief and buttoned up his trousers beneath the blanket.

As they lined up to go bathe, Colin stole glances at Patrick. Patrick acted the same as ever, as if nothing extraordinary had taken place only minutes before. Up on the decks, Patrick joined his group and Colin had to stay with his. He washed himself thoroughly, his cock tingling as he brushed it under the shallow water in the metal basin.

Then it was time for breakfast, and then back up on deck for their morning exercise. Patrick joined his friends, and Colin stood at the ship's rail, telling himself not to let it bother him. He knew he couldn't expect anything from Patrick, but he'd been with another man, and it had been incredible. Empowering.

As the day went on, Colin's stomach somersaulted agreeably when he remembered the pleasures brought by Patrick's mouth. The tenderness of his touch. For the first time, Colin looked forward to the darkness. After dinner, he waited in his bunk as the others milled about. Patrick returned as the lights were downed.

He gave Colin a smile. "Sleep well, Lord."

Slumber was the last thing on Colin's mind. "I thought perhaps…"

Patrick chuckled. "Did you now?"

A guard approached, and Patrick disappeared onto his bunk. After a moment, Colin heard his whisper. "Sleep."

Colin sighed, disappointed. He knew the risks and the punishment they faced if caught, but he craved Patrick's closeness. He snaked his hand down below his waistband, and he stroked himself to completion, fantasies running through his mind. Then he slept peacefully.

The next afternoon, Reverend Sewell approached as Colin strolled around the perimeter of the deck. "You're looking well, Colin. I'm glad of it."

"Am I? Thank you." The good reverend would surely be shocked to know one of the reasons for Colin's improved bearing. "You know, I've decided to take your counsel."

"Glad to hear it! Er, which aspect in particular?"

"Letting go of the past." Colin wasn't going to let anyone make him ashamed. He was done with nightmares.

"Ah, yes. It can be a powerful thing."

After the reverend left, Colin looked out at the endless horizon, where his future lay. He vowed that he would greet it at the ready, with eyes open.

Chapter Six

AFTER TWO MONTHS at sea, Colin had become accustomed to the constant hunger. Their rations were enough to keep them alive and in what Dr. Fairfowl referred to as "satisfactory health." But there was never enough food to fill Colin's belly and sate his appetite.

When he remembered the veritable feasts he'd enjoyed at home, Colin realized he'd never begun to appreciate his good fortune. The last meal he'd had with his family, the night of the fateful party, had been an exquisite roast beef. He wished he'd savored it more. He was determined to savor life's little pleasures whenever he could.

Breathing the salty air deeply, Colin leaned on the ship's rail. The endless ocean surrounded the *Lady Harewood*. As Patrick came to stand alongside him, Colin suppressed a smile. Although—much to his disappointment—they'd had no further physical relations, they were certainly on friendlier terms. For the most part, Patrick passed the time with his Irishmen, and Colin spent his hours alone or with Reverend Sewell, who had become a friend of a sort. But at times Patrick and Colin would converse, just the two of them.

"It's amazing, isn't it?" Colin asked.

"What?"

"This." Colin waved his arm. "The ocean. The vastness of it

all. England seems such a speck in comparison."

"Aye. It does."

A woman's gay laugh wafted down from the upper deck. Colin watched her contentedly. She was petite and blonde, older but still beautiful. She'd attracted the attention of many of the convicts, whose gazes were hungry. A man Colin assumed to be her husband appeared to be telling a humorous tale.

Colin mused aloud. "I wonder why they're going to Australia. They're not prisoners, clearly."

Patrick glanced over his shoulder at the couple. "Probably think it'll be a romantic adventure. Taming a wild land."

"Perhaps it will be."

Patrick scoffed. "Life doesn't generally turn out the way you'd imagine."

"Really? I hadn't realized," Colin noted dryly.

"They're fools."

Colin looked back. The man kissed his wife's cheek affectionately. "They're in love."

"*Love*. Spare me. Love is a game people play to get what they want. Nothing more."

"Such a cynic!" Colin had to laugh.

"A realist, Lord Lancaster. Naught but a realist."

"And what do you know of love? How can you be so sure?" A thought occurred. "Have you ever been in love yourself?"

"Of course not." Yet Patrick wouldn't meet Colin's eyes.

"You *have*!" Colin could hardly believe it.

Patrick stared out to sea and didn't answer.

"You must tell me now. You brought it up."

Patrick shrugged. "I was young and foolish once too."

"*And?*"

"And I learned love is nothing more than an illusion."

"Well, go on. We're at sea for two months to come, and there's precious little else to discuss. Might as well fill the time."

After a few moments of silence, Patrick relented. "He was the blacksmith in our village. Outside Belfast. He took me on as an apprentice when I was seventeen. Soon he was teaching me a sight more than just shoeing horses."

The thought alone made Colin's breeches tighten. "And then?"

Patrick stared out at the waves. "He filled my head with nonsense. Told me he'd leave his wife and children. That we'd go to England together."

Colin felt a stab of jealousy at the thought of Patrick with another man—another man he cared for. "Did you?"

"No. I went to England on my own."

"He couldn't go through with it? I imagine leaving one's children would be—"

"For God's sake, he was never going to leave them." Patrick laughed bitterly. "All his talk of love was simply to keep me pliable and willing. He never meant a word."

"I'm sure he did. He must have." *How could he not?*

"Really? You're so positive?"

"I…" Colin faltered.

"I had to leave my position, of course. Once I confronted him and realized it was all a lie. A year of training and strenuous work in that smithy, all for naught."

"Couldn't you have apprenticed elsewhere?"

"If the bastard hadn't told everyone I was a lying thief. Couldn't get a job anywhere after that gossip made the rounds. Figured I might as well go to England." He absently twisted the tarnished metal band on his right ring finger.

"What did your parents think?"

He shrugged. "What could they say? My older brother was a successful stonemason with a wife and children. I was a bitter disappointment."

Colin motioned to the band of metal on Patrick's finger. He'd wondered about it before, surprised the guards had allowed him to keep it. "Was that from him?"

Patrick blinked in genuine surprise. "God, no. Wouldn't want a thing that charlatan had touched." He opened his hand, gazing at the band. "It was my grandfather's. Little more than tin, really. He gave it to me just before I left. Said he knew I was no thief, and that I'd make something of my life." Patrick scoffed. "Glad he can't see me now. Glad none of them can."

"It's not too late. To make something of your life. And to...find someone. Someone who'll love you as you deserve."

Patrick shook his head. "One day you'll learn, just as I did. Everyone lets you down sooner or later. There's no love for our kind. We men take our pleasure and move on. If you want sonnets and rose petals, you'd better find yourself a wife."

With that, Patrick strode off, his long legs taking him swiftly across the deck. The woman laughed again, but Colin kept his eyes on the horizon. Perhaps Patrick was right, and love was something Colin would never have. He was quite sorry he'd brought it up.

As THEY SAILED down the African coast after stopping briefly in the West Indies, the weather had become unaccountably cold. In the early morning, Colin shivered in the darkness, unable to go back to sleep. The belly of the ship was either freezing or sweltering, and no happy medium seemed possible. As they crossed the ocean, the weather had varied considerably. With well over a hundred men living atop one another, the stench in the heat was unbearable.

Yet as the chill seeped in, Colin wished fervently for warmth, no matter what unpleasantness accompanied it. Colin couldn't imagine how convicts had survived the journey in years past when they'd been confined below for the entire voyage. As it was, they spent countless hours locked in the ship's hold.

The crew and passengers slept in cabins on the mid deck, and Colin wondered what their quarters were like. The thought that he'd be without privacy for years to come was not a happy one, to say the least. He didn't dwell, however. There was nothing he could do to change his circumstances, and he would make the best of them.

Colin switched to his other side on the hard bunk, curling up to retain what heat he could. The worn blanket did little to provide comfort or warmth. Even after lights blazed, signaling morning, he remained abed. A few minutes later, a guard's voice bellowed through the barracks. "Yer stayin' in today. Too cold up top."

This news was greeted with some grumbles, but like Colin, it seemed most of the other men didn't fancy being outside in such dire temperatures. The wind could be heard howling, and Colin could only imagine how frigid it would be on the main deck.

Although he had never really liked his lessons with old Mr. Wheeldon, on the ship he'd often wished for his textbooks to read. At least outside, the passage of the hours was tolerable. Stuck in the hold, the minutes crawled by.

The thought of textbooks brought the painful realization that William would be matriculating at Cambridge now. Colin had never felt so removed from that world. It amazed him to think he would be there too, if things had gone differently. If he'd held his tongue.

Yet no matter how bad things were as a convict, so far Colin still felt relieved that his secret was out. He wondered how he'd feel in a year's time, and what his life would be like. He couldn't even begin to imagine—it was a blank in his mind.

After breakfast, many men slept, while others played invented games with buttons as playing chips. A few others got into a brawl and had to be separated by the furious guards, who promised them punishment would be coming. A few men had gotten the lash already for stealing extra rations. All the convicts had been forced to watch, and Colin had felt sick to his stomach at the horrifying and bloody display.

Still others came together furtively to slake their bodies' desires. Their couplings were swift and harsh from what Colin could tell, carried out in the ship's darkest corners, as far from the guards' eyes and ears as possible.

Colin wondered if they had any affection for each other. Were they like him and Patrick, and would choose men over women in any case? Or were they just taking what they could? He suspected it was the latter for most.

When he woke the following morning, Colin's teeth chattered. There would be no going outside on this day, he knew. Nature called, and he reluctantly thrust his blanket aside and clambered down. He often tried to make it to the water closet before the others woke. While he was used to the utter lack of privacy, he certainly didn't like it.

The water closet was a foul-smelling part of the hold no matter what the temperature. There was no screen, simply a low, wooden partition and a seat over a stained bowl that led to the sea. Colin did his business quickly and returned to his bunk. He wasn't sure of the time but hoped it wouldn't be long before breakfast, as his stomach rumbled. Without seeing daylight, he found time began to play tricks. For all he knew, it could still be the middle of the night.

Carefully, Colin placed his boot on the edge of Patrick's bunk. Once he'd trod on Patrick's hand, which had not been appreciated in the slightest.

"Bloody freezing," Patrick whispered.

Colin always felt a silly little thrill when Patrick initiated a conversation. Although there had been no rancor between them as the voyage had gone on, it seemed to Colin as if Patrick was determined to keep him at arm's length.

After a moment's consideration, Colin snatched his blanket from his berth and gave Patrick a nudge. Surprisingly, Patrick shifted over without comment. They spread both their blankets over them and huddled underneath, bodies pressed close. "At least it'll be hot in Australia," Colin said. "So I hear."

Patrick chuckled. "Aye. Too bad we'll be digging ditches in that heat."

Colin had assumed they'd be kept away in cells. "Labor? We won't simply be locked up?"

"No. From what I've heard, they're using prisoners to build their towns. Digging, clearing rocks, constructing roads. It's a vast land with hardly any people. Not compared to home, at least. We'll have our work cut out for us."

Colin pondered it. "It's better than rotting in a cell, I think."

"That it is. I just hope there's food. I'm starving on this damn ship."

"What I wouldn't give for an apple. Straight off the tree."

"Stop; we'll both jump overboard and swim for the nearest land if we think on food too much."

Colin chuckled and inched closer to Patrick. He longed to be touched again, to feel Patrick's hands and mouth on his flesh once more. He boldly reached down to stroke Patrick's thigh. "So cold."

Patrick's voice was low and went straight to Colin's cock. "Guess it won't do any harm to warm ourselves up."

Before he could answer, Patrick urged Colin to lie atop him, pulling him close. Colin's heart pounded as he settled on Patrick, their bodies lining up. Patrick's cold hands stole down the back of Colin's trousers, which had loosened as he lost weight due to the paltry rations.

Colin ground down, thrusting his pelvis as Patrick squeezed

Colin's ass. Although they were separated by the coarse fabric of their uniforms, the friction was delicious. Soon they were both hard as they rocked together, breathing fast as the pressure built.

He sought Patrick's lips, but Patrick turned his head sharply. After the flash of disappointment, Colin contented himself with kissing Patrick's neck, sucking the tender skin at the crease of Patrick's shoulder as they rutted against each other. For so long, Colin had yearned to be with another man—to be with Patrick. The heat of Patrick's body and the sound of his harsh breaths and grunts aroused Colin to new heights.

They writhed together, bucking and straining, their breath frosting the frigid air. Colin came first, his face buried in Patrick's neck as he moaned. He knew his trousers would be uncomfortably sticky, but it was worth the small price for the intense pleasure. Patrick tightened his fingers on Colin's buttocks, and he thrust upward until he groaned and spilled. They both breathed heavily, limbs tangled in the cramped space, Colin splayed on Patrick, flushed and content.

After a few minutes, Patrick withdrew his hands from Colin's trousers and gave his rear a pat. When Colin didn't move, Patrick prodded him lightly. Colin wished he could stay and curl up with Patrick, but he knew he was being dismissed. He longed to hear some kind words—or any words, really.

Finally, Patrick spoke. "We're warmed up. Better get back to your bed."

"But we'll be cold again in no time."

Patrick laughed quietly. "I've created a monster."

Colin moved to kiss Patrick, who dodged again. His smile disappeared. "If we're cold later, then we'll find other companions when the guards aren't looking. There are plenty willing here."

"Have you? With others?" Colin was struck with hurt and jealousy.

"Of course," Patrick answered quickly. "It doesn't mean anything. *This* doesn't mean anything."

"But…"

Patrick grasped Colin's waist with his strong hands, and he lifted him off. Colin grabbed hold of his blanket and escaped to the upper bunk. He scolded himself for being a fool. Of course it meant nothing to Patrick. He just wished it was nothing to him as well. Instead it felt like everything.

AFTER FOUR FREEZING days and nights trapped in the belly of the ship, Colin thought he'd go mad from the boredom and claustrophobia. He and Patrick had barely spoken, a new rift between them. He didn't care if it was arctic outside—he needed fresh air. Needed to get outside and see the sun. The convicts were restless without their daily exercise, and tempers flared.

By midday, Colin thought it seemed a bit warmer, but wasn't sure if it was his imagination. However the next morning, they were finally allowed back up on deck in shifts to bathe. It was still brisk and the bathwater was glacial, but Colin reveled in being clean again.

In the following days, the prisoners' routine returned to normal. Colin walked with Reverend Sewell, who insisted that Colin call him by his given name of Richard when they were alone. He talked of his plans for eventually building a new church in the Australian desert. Colin enjoyed listening to Richard's grand ideas. He hoped they'd come to fruition.

When Colin woke one morning later that week, he found the heat had most decidedly returned. Or that the ship had sailed into it, more accurately. Everyone had begun to stir, and Colin hopped down from his bunk. Patrick murmured and kicked at his blanket, which was already balled up and tangled around his feet.

"Guess we shouldn't have complained about the temperature,"

Colin noted wryly.

There was no reply from Patrick, and Colin sighed, frustrated. "You can't even speak to me at all now?"

Only silence. Colin leaned down and gave Patrick's shoulder a forceful shake. He touched fevered, slick skin, and his breath caught. "Patrick?" Colin tried to rouse him, his alarm growing with each moment, but Patrick only muttered, eyelids fluttering. When Colin pressed the back of his hand to Patrick's forehead, his stomach twisted into a knot.

Colin darted up the narrow aisle to the bars separating the barracks from the guards' station in the center of the deck. "You must fetch the doctor! Hurry!"

The guard manning the watch was Ford, who strode to the bars. "You speak only when spoken to!" he barked.

"Please. I'm sorry. My friend is ill. He's burning up."

Ford lowered his voice. "Half the crew and settlers are ill. The doctor will be down when he's seen to them. Don't hold your breath."

Colin's panic deepened. "What is it?"

"Looks like typhoid."

Colin's heart thumped painfully. *Oh, God. No.* "How?"

"However it happens. I'm no doctor. Now get back to your bunk and stay there. No one's going up today."

"Please, when the doctor comes, send him right over."

There were footfalls on the wooden stairs from the deck above, and Ford stepped away from the bars. "Get back now or he'll be the last one the doctor sees," he hissed.

Colin dashed away. On his way back into the barracks, he looked closely at the other convicts, noting several other men who appeared sickened. Patrick remained in the grip of the fever, seemingly unaware of Colin's presence. Colin had a small portion of his water ration from the previous day remaining, and he tried to tip it into Patrick's mouth. Most dribbled down his chin, but

Colin hoped he swallowed a little.

Colin belatedly realized that the water could be the source of the illness. He didn't drink any himself, although he was powerfully thirsty. Word of the outbreak spread rapidly, and no rations came that day. Patrick's temperature soared so frighteningly high that Colin feared it would kill him.

As the day dragged on, Colin stayed at Patrick's side, perched on the edge of the bunk. He'd stripped off Patrick's shirt and trousers to make him more comfortable, leaving him only in his drawers. He spoke to Patrick in low tones, hoping the other man could hear him. He talked of nothing, really, just rambling nonsense and stories and whatever popped into his mind. He was afraid if he stopped talking, Patrick would simply slip away in the silence.

Dr. Fairfowl finally appeared late in the day. He was utterly exhausted, and dark circles stood out under his eyes. He conducted a cursory exam of Patrick, who was still lost to the fever world. Colin hovered nearby anxiously.

The doctor straightened and spoke to the guard accompanying him. "Another one. No food until the fever breaks."

Colin waited for the doctor to administer some kind of medicine to Patrick, but he didn't. Colin was speaking before he knew what he was doing. "That will cure it?" Colin was shaky and parched and couldn't imagine how weak Patrick would become with no nourishment.

Dr. Fairfowl glanced at Colin. "Perhaps. There's no treatment to speak of. It spreads through the water or food. Some won't get sick at all. Some will die. Some will live. If he's strong, he might be one of the lucky ones." With that, he turned away.

Colin clasped hold of the doctor's arm. "Wait! There must be something you can do!"

The blow landed so suddenly across the side of his head that Colin was on the floor before he could process it. The guard towered over him, his face a twisted snarl. "Touch 'im again and it's the lash for you."

Colin's ear rang for the rest of the day. He stayed by Patrick's side until exhaustion and hunger forced him to take to his own bunk to rest. The heat in the barracks was oppressive, and sweat dripped from every man, not just those trapped in the throes of the fever.

They were told the water supply was being purified. Colin's tongue became swollen in his mouth, and his throat felt as if it had been coated in sand. He fervently hoped the water ration would come soon.

Just before curfew, they were allowed a small amount of water each. Colin told himself to sip it, but he couldn't help but gulp greedily. Patrick remained unconscious, moaning and thrashing from time to time. Colin sat by his side, talking to him once more in a low voice.

When no one seemed to be looking, he stroked Patrick's hair, which was soaked with sweat. Colin had never felt so helpless in all his years. He'd felt similarly when he'd feared for Patrick's life after Patrick was discovered as a sodomite, but at least then he'd been able to do something to help him.

He still couldn't explain the hold Patrick had over him, but it had only grown stronger. Especially after the intimacies they'd shared, even if Patrick declared them meaningless. Colin didn't seem to have the ability to separate his emotions from the physical acts. He wondered if he'd feel differently with another man, but the thought of being intimate with anyone but Patrick was both frightening and unappealing.

The lights were doused, but Colin stayed perched on the edge of Patrick's bunk. With no one able to see them, he boldly took hold of Patrick's hand, squeezing tightly, hoping to penetrate the feverish haze. "You're strong. You're going to make it." *You must.* Colin stroked the dull metal of the tarnished ring Patrick wore on his right ring finger.

For a moment, Colin swore Patrick's fingers tightened on his, but it passed and Colin could invoke no further response. He leaned over and pressed a kiss to Patrick's flushed forehead. Then, unable to resist, Colin brushed their lips together, the barest touch.

The bobbing lantern of a guard on rounds appeared, and Colin quickly hoisted himself up onto his own bed. He fell into a restless sleep and dreamed of riding, Patrick's strong arms around him.

WHEN PATRICK'S FEVER finally broke, Colin could hardly believe it. For the first time in endless days, Patrick gazed at him with clear, focused eyes. It was midmorn, and most of the other convicts were on the main deck for their exercise. Those that remained in the barracks were the ill, save for Colin and the guards. Colin had ventured above decks a few times but had worried too much about Patrick and had returned swiftly.

Patrick blinked dozily. "Are we there yet?" His voice was barely a croak.

Colin's heart soared at the attempt at humor. "I hope so. It's certainly hot enough."

Patrick tried to reply but wheezed instead. Colin helped him lift his head and wrapped an arm around his shoulders before tipping a flask to Patrick's lips. He choked at first but was able to get some of the water down before lying back, seemingly exhausted by the effort expended.

Patrick soon slept again and woke only to drink more water and then sleep again. His skin cooled somewhat, and Colin breathed a deep sigh of relief. The next morning, when the lanterns were lit and Colin hopped down from his bunk, he found

Patrick sitting on his berth, leaning back against the wooden hull.

"Morning." Patrick's voice was markedly stronger.

Colin grinned. "Good morning. You seem much improved." He sat on the side of the bed.

"Aye. What was it? This sickness?"

"Typhoid. It was in the water, they think. Everything's been boiled now, or so we hope."

"Jesus. No wonder I feel as if I've been dragged behind a stallion for days."

Colin had heard whispers of the number of dead and had noticed several bunks were now empty in the barracks. "You're lucky to be alive. Some of the settlers and a few of us weren't so lucky. A couple of crew members too."

"I suppose I have you to thank for that."

"Me?" Colin shrugged. "You fought it off yourself."

"Still. Thank you."

"No need." Colin found he was blushing under Patrick's gaze.

A guard shouted for the men in Colin's group to assemble for their march above decks to bathe. With a parting smile, Colin fell into step with the others. He imagined he could feel Patrick's gaze on him all the way up to the main deck.

PATRICK'S HEALTH IMPROVED with each passing day as they neared their destination. They had stopped at the Cape of Good Hope at the southern tip of Africa, but the men had not been allowed above decks while in port, much to their disgruntlement. Now they sailed across the Indian Ocean, ever closer to Australia.

There was still a sense of the absurd to Colin's life on the ship. As much as he'd become acclimated to his uncomfortable and at times menacing surroundings, he'd catch himself imagining he'd see William or his family again soon. He couldn't even conjure up an image of what Australia might be like in his mind. It was a complete and utter mystery.

His life in England seemed years behind him. Colin wondered how Will was enjoying Cambridge and if he'd made the rowing squad. Rebecca would be doing her studies and obsessively planning her society debut, although it wouldn't happen for at least another year. She'd designed her dream gown countless times and likely would countless more before the event.

Too many thoughts of home drew Colin into a funk, and he tried to keep his focus on the future. Of course, too many thoughts of what might await him in an unknown land didn't do much to improve his mood. Reverend Sewell advised him to keep his mind on the present, but considering he was living in fetid, deplorable conditions, it wasn't much comfort. The heat was extreme, the air in the barracks stifling.

All in all, thirty people had died from the typhoid, and they'd of course been buried at sea. The prisoners were only present for the service for the group of convicts who had succumbed, although Colin noticed several settlers watching from the upper deck.

As the reverend spoke of eternal life, Colin's attention was drawn to the blonde woman he'd noticed previously. Her face was pale and grim, and she wore black. The man he'd seen teasing her so joyfully was no longer at her side. Although Colin didn't even know her name, he felt a pang of sorrow for her loss.

Once the bodies were overboard, the ship returned to its normal schedule of daily activities as if nothing had happened. Colin wasn't sure if God was listening, but he said a silent prayer of thanks that Patrick wasn't sinking into the abyss of the ocean.

That night, the ship lurched from side to side on the heavy seas, and Colin was grateful his stomach had long become accustomed to the motion. Still, keeping his footing was a challenge, and he stumbled in the narrow passage between the rows of bunks. Before he could crack his knee on the sharp wooden corner of a berth, strong hands caught him about the waist from behind.

For a moment, Colin thrashed, terror flooding his veins, but he realized it was Patrick. He took a deep breath. "Thank you." He staggered again as the ship rode another wave.

"Lights out!" The guard's yell boomed through the hold, and a moment later the lanterns were doused.

In the darkness, Colin stumbled forward, the only light coming from the guards' station beyond the iron bars in the center of the deck. Patrick's hands stayed firm on Colin's waist, and when they reached their bunk, instead of letting go, Patrick unexpectedly pulled Colin down with him onto his narrow bed.

A thrill of desire and excitement set Colin's heart racing. "You *are* feeling better."

Patrick's breath warmed his ear. "Still alive. Might as well celebrate, eh?" Their bodies pressed together, but Patrick seemed to be waiting for a response.

Colin whispered, "Yes."

As soon as the word was uttered, Patrick roamed his hands over Colin's body, snaking beneath his clothing, undoing buttons. With so many men around them and the guards on watch, Colin was careful to keep quiet, even as Patrick squeezed Colin's cock with his warm palm.

Colin's eyes hadn't adjusted to the dark yet, but as Patrick tugged his hips to the edge of the bunk, he realized Patrick had gone on his knees on the floor in the narrow aisle. Any man up after the lights were out would walk straight into him. Patrick spread Colin's legs, and the wet heat of his mouth covered Colin's cock.

Reaching out, Colin's fingers tangled in Patrick's hair as he jerked in delight. As opposed to the first time Patrick had pleasured him like this, there was no gentleness. Patrick's mouth suctioned tightly, and he bobbed up and down, squeezing and twisting his hand around the base of Colin's cock as he sucked forcefully.

The roughness was a new and powerful sensation, and Colin couldn't stop a moan from escaping. It had been a revelation that men pleasured each other with their mouths, and now he was learning it could be as carnal as he imagined it would be to have Patrick inside him, riding him.

Colin thrust his hips up into the heat of Patrick's mouth, his entire body ablaze. He bit his lip to remain silent. Sweat dripped down his neck, and he struggled to breathe in the muggy air as Patrick took him deep into his throat. Being pleasured like that, his legs spread wide, Colin felt utterly wanton. When Patrick touched Colin's bollocks, he spilled his seed in a rush of intense pleasure. Patrick swallowed every burst, milking Colin until he was empty.

Panting, he lay back and promptly thwacked his head on the rough, wooden planks of the ship's hull. As Patrick joined him on the narrow bunk, he stifled his laughter and rubbed the back of Colin's head lightly. Colin had to smile himself. When the pain receded, he shimmied down to the end of the bed, eager to taste Patrick in turn. He'd imagined it for weeks on end, and no headache would make him pass up the opportunity.

With several yanks, Patrick's shoes and pants came off. Colin could see outlines in the dark now, and Patrick bent his legs, spreading them wide with his feet flat on the hard bunk. Although Colin had just spent himself, desire rippled through him anew.

Heart thumping, he took Patrick in hand, stroking him tentatively, reveling in the sensation of the heated flesh of another man beneath his touch. After a deep breath, Colin bent down and sought Patrick with his mouth. His teeth scraped the sensitive flesh, and Patrick hissed. Colin slowed himself and took care to cover his teeth with his upper lip as he tasted Patrick again. He explored tentatively, tracing the contours of Patrick's thick, throbbing cock with his tongue.

The musky scent and taste were as intoxicating as any wine Colin had tasted. Patrick lightly guided Colin's head lower. When Colin went too far and choked, Patrick brushed his hair back and murmured something Colin couldn't make out.

After a deep breath, Colin explored farther and tried to establish a rhythm with his mouth and tongue. He hoped he was catching the hang of it and thought Patrick's increasingly erratic breathing as the minutes went by was a good sign. He could feel Patrick's pulse thrumming through his cock, and it filled Colin's senses.

When Colin increased the pressure of his lips, Patrick bucked up. With one hand, Colin massaged Patrick's bollocks as he sucked harder. After a few more seconds of this, Patrick pulled Colin's head up and came, splashing his own stomach and Colin's chin.

Colin darted his tongue out to taste the droplets near his mouth, and he decided that next time—because there *had* to be a next time—he would like to swallow every last drop. Patrick's legs flopped down, and Colin fit himself against Patrick's side.

Suddenly a gruff voice came from across the aisle. "If you're done wit' him, I'll take a turn."

Patrick's body tensed. "You'll take a step closer to a watery grave," he growled.

The man chuckled. "Never hurts to ask, does it?"

Colin waited for Patrick to send him back to his upper bunk, but instead he wrapped his arm around Colin's shoulders. A few minutes later, Patrick snored lightly, and Colin grinned into the darkness.

Chapter Seven

As the *Lady Harewood* sailed below Australia to reach the port of Sydney on the eastern side, they could see land in the distance. At first, the men crowded about the railing of the ship, eager for a glimpse of their new home. Soon they realized all that met the eye were dense forests and foreboding, rocky headlands. It cooled their excitement considerably.

On deck one afternoon, the captain called for order. Surveying the convicts, he waited so long to speak that Colin was sure he was only doing it for dramatic effect. The sun beat down overhead, and Colin edged his way to the shade below one of the ship's masts. He spent much of his time on deck trying to prevent his skin from being fried.

The captain finally spoke. "If the seas are on our side, tomorrow we shall reach Sydney Cove."

There was a murmur among the men and the settlers who stood on the upper deck, along with the captain. One of the children clapped joyfully, prompting laughter from many. Surprisingly the captain didn't seem to mind. He waited until he had all eyes on him once more. "Upon our arrival, we will be met by the colonial secretary, the chief superintendent of convicts, and other officials."

He surveyed the prisoners solemnly. "Your fate rests in these men's hands. Once they decide on an appropriate course of action, you will begin your new lives in service to the colony. May God have mercy on your souls."

The captain strode away, and the men talked quietly among themselves. Staying in the shade, Colin sat and contemplated the future, which, after months of waiting, was suddenly on the horizon.

"May I join you?"

Colin looked up to find Reverend Sewell standing over him. He glanced about to ensure no one was listening before calling him by name. "Hello, Richard. Yes, please do."

The reverend sat. He wore a wide-brimmed hat that protected his fair skin, although his ginger freckles stood out more strongly than ever. "How are you feeling now that we've almost arrived?"

"I'm not sure. Apprehensive. A little excited. Very glad to be getting off this ship."

Richard chuckled. "That makes two of us. I've had my fill of the seafaring life."

"You don't think you'll ever go back?"

"To England? No. No, I don't imagine I will."

"It's just all so…final."

"Yes, I suppose it is." Richard clasped Colin's shoulder. "Don't worry. You'll find your way. God has a plan."

"I hope his plan agrees with that of the superintendent of convicts."

As Richard squeezed Colin's shoulder encouragingly, Colin noticed Patrick watching them from twenty feet away. Richard followed his gaze and took in Patrick's glare. "That's the man you were brought here with, isn't it?"

They'd never discussed the nature of Colin's crime nor any of the other details of how he'd ended up a convict. "Yes. I've known him for years. We were friends once." He had no idea what they were now. A few more times, they'd come together at night for furtive groping. In the day they carried on as normal, as if nothing happened between them in the darkness. Colin never knew where he stood.

"He seems discontent."

Patrick turned away from their gazes, and Colin watched him disappear into the crowd. "I don't know what he feels." Just the night before, Colin had moved to kiss him as they'd rutted against each other. Patrick would never allow it, always turning his face away.

"I'm sure you'll make new friends soon. You won't be a prisoner forever. With good behavior, you could have your freedom in only a few years."

A few years. It seemed a lifetime. "Yes, perhaps."

"You'll have to look me up and join my parish." Richard smiled.

Colin decided to ask the question he'd been wondering since he'd met the reverend. "Doesn't it bother you? The fact that I'm a criminal? That I'm a sodomite?"

Richard paled slightly. "Please don't use that word."

"But it's who I am."

"That's not true!" Richard took hold of Colin's forearm, squeezing as he spoke intently. "You can overcome your nature. With God's help, you can be a better person. A righteous man."

"I don't think so." Colin tried to withdraw his arm, but Richard held fast. "At least not in the way you see it."

"Yes, you can. I *know* it. I myself—" He stopped suddenly and seemed to engage in a fierce internal debate. After a few moments, he sat back and his hands fell to his lap. "You must pray to the Lord for strength, Colin. Pray for his guidance to lead you to salvation."

Colin thought of the relief he'd felt when his secret had been revealed. Of the pleasure he'd found in Patrick's arms. "I don't think my salvation is the same as others'."

Richard took on the tone he used for sermons. "Of course it is.

With the Lord's help, we can—"

"Change?"

"Yes. *Change.*" Richard nodded encouragingly.

"The thing is, I don't *want* to change."

Richard's smile faded. "Of course you do. You need to repent. To atone for your sins. We all do."

"A sin could never feel so natural. So *right.*"

"I know it may seem that way, but trust me, you must seek a righteous path. I fear for your soul, Colin. You're so much better than the rest of these men. You're special."

"I do seek my path, Richard. But I don't think I shall find you on it. I don't want to *change* the man I am. I want to discover him."

Richard's face was rigid. "You must school your aberrant desires. Only then will you find happiness and purpose. Only then."

Colin imagined a life of repressing his desires as he had for the last three years. It was unthinkable. Resolved, he stood. "Thank you for your friendship and counsel, Richard. I hope you find what you're looking for in Australia."

"Colin, wait!"

As Colin wove through the other men on the deck, he didn't look back.

COLIN'S STOMACH GROWLED as curfew approached. He lay on his bunk, trousers rolled to the knees and shirt undone to try and get even a bit of relief from the heat. Being slick with sweat had become normal, as had being constantly hungry. After the typhoid outbreak, their rations had been only the remaining salt pork and beef stores, and the hunger was pervasive.

"Last night." Patrick stood beside the bunk, his shirt hanging open as well. Although he'd lost weight on the voyage and especially due to the sickness, Colin still found himself admiring the planes of Patrick's chest.

"Hard to believe, isn't it?"

"Aye." Patrick ran his hand through his hair, which had become quite shaggy. They were all in desperate need of a cut. "Suppose you'll miss your friend."

"Who?" Then it occurred to him. "Oh, you mean Richard?"

"*Richard*, is it? Surprised he hasn't arranged for some private prayers for the two of you tonight."

Colin was puzzled by Patrick's rancor. "Private? I don't think that's permitted. Besides, he doesn't say much differently to me than he does in his sermons. He means well, but I don't think he can help me."

"He wants to help himself to you," Patrick scoffed.

"Reverend Sewell? Wants *me*?" Colin laughed, disbelieving. "He's only being friendly."

Patrick rolled his eyes. "I don't know how you're going to get along without me if you can't tell when someone is after your tight little arse."

At the thought of being separated the next day, Colin was suddenly serious. He pushed aside all thoughts of Richard. "I don't know how I'll get along without you either."

"To bed!" a guard's voice bellowed. The lights faded throughout the hold a few moments later.

As the darkness descended, Patrick unexpectedly hoisted himself up onto Colin's berth. He rolled atop Colin, and Colin's body responded immediately. Their hands roamed, and Colin relished Patrick's weight pressing him down. He wished ardently that they had the freedom to truly mate together, that he could experience Patrick inside him.

As Patrick stroked him, he explored the side of Colin's neck with his mouth. He whispered, "You'll get by. Keep your head down, and treat everyone with suspicion. *Everyone*."

Colin panted softly and reached for Patrick, quickly opening his trousers and squeezing him. He wanted to beg Patrick to stay with him, even though he knew the decision was out of their hands. Even if sent to the same prison, they might never see each other. The labor crews would likely be scattered throughout the colony.

They rubbed their cocks together, and Patrick took them both in his large hand, their skin slick. The divine pleasure built, and Colin imagined he was bent over, Patrick's cock inside him, filling him, completing him. He thrust up into Patrick's hand and spilled, a cry escaping his lips.

They couldn't prolong their pleasure, as the fear of being caught always hung overhead. Patrick grunted and came a few moments later, his face in Colin's neck. They remained tangled in each other's arms, chests rising rapidly. Colin tightened his arms around Patrick's back. He never wanted to let go.

After their few minutes of indulgence, Patrick raised his head. Colin could barely see his expression, and his fingers traced Patrick's face as if memorizing it. Patrick spoke softly. "You're stronger than you think, Colin."

It was the first time in years that Patrick had called him by name, and Colin liked the sound very, very much. Holding Patrick's face in his hands, he leaned up and pressed their lips together. For the first time, Patrick didn't turn. He kissed Colin gently. Then he rolled away and was gone.

WHEN COLIN WOKE the following morning, it took him a moment to work out what was unsettling him. He realized the ship was at a standstill. The air was as stifling as ever, and without the motion of the sea, it seemed even more oppressive. Patrick's bunk was empty, and Colin knew a moment of fear that he was already gone and off to some far-off corner of the colony.

Happily, he soon realized all the convicts were still in the barracks. When they were allowed up to bathe, there was a barber waiting. They each took a turn in a hard-backed chair as their hair was mercifully sheared. The barber left them all with just a couple of inches of hair, and Colin was quite relieved to say good-bye to the shag that had constantly been in his eyes of late.

As he washed himself, Colin took in the view of Sydney from the ship's deck. Buildings lined the cove and what appeared to be the entire town spread out behind. He could see narrow streets and buildings, a sprawling city much bigger and quite a lot more civilized than he'd expected. Perhaps Australia wasn't such an untamed land after all.

They were all herded back down below for breakfast rations, and then they waited. And waited, and waited. The hours crawled by. Men talked quietly or returned to their bunks to sleep. Tension filled the air as they wondered what their fates would be.

As the afternoon wore on, the apprehension turned to frustration and anger that they were being kept at bay unduly. Just before dinnertime, a guard shouted for attention and informed them that they weren't going anywhere on this day. There was much grumbling in response, and the guards forced the prisoners to return to their bunks. The jailors patrolled the narrow aisles, ready to quash any rebellion.

That night, Colin thought about sneaking to Patrick's berth, but just as he was about to slip down, he heard someone coming and pretended to be sleeping. Through his lashes he saw the form of a guard pass by. The last thing he or Patrick needed was to be caught together on their last night on the ship, so Colin resolutely closed his eyes and willed himself to sleep.

The next day, thank goodness, there was a whirlwind of activity as the convicts were split into their usual groups and taken to different areas of the ship to be interviewed by an official. A man

Colin assumed to be the superintendent chatted with the captain on the upper deck. Colin could see no sign of the settlers and assumed they had been ferried to shore the day before.

He waited anxiously for his turn. Colin couldn't spot Patrick from where he stood and wondered if there was any rhyme or reason to how they were being interviewed and if which official they met in particular had a bearing on their fate.

The sun bore down, and Colin shuddered to imagine what summer would be like if this was spring weather. He'd heard the seasons were back to front in this corner of the world and that as they neared Christmas, it would become hotter and hotter.

Colin was still ten men away from the front of his line when the guard named Ford appeared at his side, his large hand tight on Colin's upper arm. "You're coming with me."

Colin was in no position to argue and fell into step as Ford led the way through the throng of men. It seemed they'd also been joined on the ship by curious locals, and the deck teemed with people. On the other side of the ship, Colin was led down into a storeroom on the mid deck.

A government official waited inside, seated at a makeshift desk of a plank of wood atop two barrels. Colin blinked in surprise when he saw Patrick standing in the corner. A ghost of a smile tugged at Patrick's lips.

The middle-aged official, who had thinning hair, a large gut and a prominent red nose, cleared his throat and seemed to stifle a belch. "Name?"

Colin waited a moment before answering, unsure if it was he who was being addressed. Ford elbowed him sharply, and Colin spoke. "Lancaster. Colin."

"Crime?"

Colin knew his face was now as red as the official's nose. "Attempted buggery."

The man said nothing and shuffled through some papers.

Finally he spoke. "Sentence to be no less than two years, and up to...well, as many years as we want to give you, really."

Not sure what his response should be, Colin glanced at Patrick, whose shoulders inched up in a tiny shrug. The official sat back in his chair, which creaked ominously. His bleary eyes met Colin's. "You're both extremely lucky you're of such low moral character."

"I..." Colin had no idea what to say.

"And why's that?" Patrick spoke up.

Ford glared and took a menacing step in Patrick's direction. "Speak when spoken to."

The official ignored them and went on. "You will both accompany one of the settlers from this ship and assist her in driving a herd of cattle inland. You will do everything and anything she orders you to."

Ford smirked. "We know the lady's virtue is safe with you two sodomites."

The official smiled for the first time, baring his yellowed teeth. "Quite. But understand that a close eye will be kept. More and more we're putting you convicts to work across the colony, but make no mistake—you are prisoners. You will obey in everything you are told to do. Be grateful for this chance to go about free of leg irons, but never forget you are captives of Australia."

Colin wasn't sure what to think about this turn of events, but his heart leaped at the news that he and Patrick would be together. As long as he was with Patrick, he didn't care what work they did or where they were sent. He glanced at Patrick, whose expression he couldn't read.

Ford led them outside and put them in a line of men waiting to be ferried to the mainland. He stayed alongside and boarded the small boat with them. The convicts were instructed to row, and Colin watched the *Lady Harewood* recede into the distance, glad to be bidding it farewell. As they sailed away, Richard appeared at the ship's rail.

"Colin!" His shout was faint.

Colin had forgotten about him and felt a pang of regret that he hadn't said a proper good-bye. Richard had been kind, even if Colin didn't agree with him on certain matters. Colin put down his oar for a moment and waved. He heard his name on the wind again, but then they were ashore. He turned and splashed onto land.

Chapter Eight

AFTER ALMOST FOUR months at sea, the sensation of walking on solid ground was a strange one, and Colin's legs felt oddly shaky as he and Patrick followed Ford up the beach and past a market, which was bustling with activity. The smell of fish was strong, and Colin's stomach growled. Oh, how he longed for a proper meal.

Ford led them some distance away, and most people seemed totally unbothered by their presence in their distinctive convict uniforms. Colin supposed they were quite used to it living in the colony.

By a modest-sized covered wagon, the small blonde woman Colin had noticed on the ship waited. She still wore black and an equally grim expression, arms crossed over her chest. Her hair was yanked back into a severe knot.

Ford smiled. "Here you are, madam, as promised. These two degenerates won't give you any trouble, and they know they're to obey you in everything. Don't be afraid to whip 'em if you feel the need."

The woman's expression didn't change. "Thank you, Mr. Ford."

He tipped his hat to her and addressed Colin and Patrick. "Be good, lads. Or you'll regret it, I promise you that."

"That's it?" Patrick's tone was strident. "We just go God

knows where with this woman?"

"What would you like, a parade to see you off? The superintendent knows exactly where you're going, and they'll be checking on you regularly. So watch your step. And your filthy Irish mouth."

Patrick's face darkened dangerously, and Colin took hold of his arm. Ford smirked and disappeared back into the crowd. The woman spoke as Patrick shook off Colin's hand. "I'm Emily Grant."

Colin and Patrick introduced themselves as Emily looked them over. She led them to the back of the wagon and pulled out a burlap sack. "There's some clothing in here for you."

"You don't want us to wear our uniforms?" Colin was pleased at the thought of being rid of the worn, rough clothing they'd donned for months on end.

"No. I don't see the need in drawing attention to you. You can ride in the back and change. We need to meet up with the herd."

Patrick eyed the two horses hitched to the wagon. "You can drive it yourself?"

Emily straightened her spine. "Yes, I can."

Patrick shrugged, and he and Colin clambered into the back of the wagon, which was covered by thick canvas over a rectangular wooden frame. As the wagon jolted and rumbled on its way, they searched through the sack.

"Must have been her husband's things," Colin whispered.

"Nah. Wouldn't sully his memory, I don't think." He indicated two large steamer trunks stored at the front of the wagon's storage area. "One of those is his, I wager. Maybe they had hired men with them. More than one of the settlers died. Must be their things."

Colin felt oddly guilty about wearing a dead man's clothing, but he shucked the uniform gratefully. He chose a blue, buttoned shirt and brown trousers, which were both a bit too big for him, but he found a belt. The clothing was soft and comfortable and quite a treat in contrast to the uniform.

In the close quarters, he watched from the corner of his eye as Patrick peeled his shirt off. "We should burn these damn things," Patrick grumbled.

Colin chuckled, and his eyes were drawn to Patrick's chest. When he finally looked up, Patrick was watching him. Patrick put on his new shirt and buttoned it.

"Don't get any ideas, Lord."

"I wasn't! I'm not."

"Right. Let's just hope the merry widow knows where she's leading us. Could be the death of us yet."

IT WAS HOURS before the wagon stopped. When Colin poked his head out from the back flap, there was no sign of civilization but the dirt road they'd traveled on. His heart sank.

They climbed out, and Colin realized the low humming sound he could hear was a herd of hundreds of cattle grazing in a clearing. In all directions, Colin could see only fields and clumps of trees.

Emily surveyed the animals silently, and a young man strode toward them. He was a bit shorter than Colin but had a muscled, lean physique. A shock of sandy hair swept back from his forehead when he neatly doffed his wide-brimmed, brown leather hat and smiled. There was a small gap between his front teeth, but somehow it added to his good looks.

The man extended his hand to Patrick. "Mr. Grant. Pleasure to meet you. I received word that the ship had arrived."

Before Patrick could respond, Emily did. "Mr. Grant is dead." Her tone brooked no argument. "These are my animals now."

The man was clearly surprised, but quickly recovered. He

stepped toward Emily, his hand still extended. "I'm Robert. Robbie, everyone calls me. I'm very sorry for your loss, Mrs. Grant."

Emily shook his hand warily. "Where is our guide?"

"You're looking at 'im, ma'am."

"*You?*" Her brow creased. "You're just a boy."

Robbie straightened. "I'm twenty-one, ma'am. And I know my way around the land and the cattle; don't worry."

"My husband was told—"

"That he'd get the best guide money can buy. I've grown up here in New South Wales. Traveled all around since I was a boy, driving cattle, ranching. I live in the saddle. You won't find better than me."

"I suppose I won't find anyone *but* you, given the shortage of labor in the colony."

Robbie shrugged. "True as that is, I'm the best. I promise you that."

"Where are the men who helped you get the cattle this far from the ranch down south? You couldn't have done it alone. There are five hundred." Emily surveyed the herd. "There *are* five hundred, correct?"

"To a one. I don't lose cattle, and I don't run 'em into the ground. Move fifteen miles or so a day, and they stay healthy. The others have gone back to make other deliveries, ma'am. There were to be three men with you. Which is more than we'd usually have with five hundred head of cattle."

Emily waved her hand in Colin and Patrick's direction. "It's just these two."

"Ah, we'll be fine. I can handle three hundred on my own."

"You're sure you know where we're going?"

"Yes, ma'am. A thousand miles northwest. It'll be a great spot for a station."

"A thousand miles?" Colin blurted. At fifteen miles a day, it would take at least two months.

"Would you rather be back behind bars?" Emily asked.

Admonished, Colin shook his head. Robbie gazed at him quizzically. "Prison, eh?"

Emily nodded at Colin and Patrick. "These are my workers." She paused. "My prisoners, I should say. They're not to be trusted. They're to take orders from you, and if they disobey, you can reprimand them as you see fit."

"Whatever you say, ma'am." Robbie flipped his hat up his arm playfully before placing it back on his head.

"Let's get on with it, then," Emily replied.

Robbie eyed them all. "Do you have the proper equipment? You'll be needing hats. The sun is stronger here than you're used to in England. Or so they tell me."

"Yes, I have a hat." Emily frowned at Colin and Patrick. "Is there a store nearby?"

"You'd have had a better selection in Sydney."

Emily seemed momentarily flustered. "Well, we were in a rush. Is there a store or not?"

"You're in luck. It's about thirty miles up the track."

"That's the closest? *Thirty* miles?"

Robbie grinned. "After that it's a hell of a lot farther, so we'd better stock up." He motioned to Colin and Patrick. "Follow me, boys. Ma'am, you'll lead in the wagon. If you're sure you can handle it?"

"*Yes.*" Emily turned on her heel and climbed up onto the wagon.

Colin and Patrick fell in step with Robbie as they headed to a tree with four horses tied to it. "Whatcha' in for?" Robbie asked.

Colin pondered briefly whether or not they should lie, but Patrick was already answering. "Buggery." He was defiant—proud, even.

Robbie's stride didn't falter, although his eyebrow rose. "That so?"

Colin spoke up. "Yes." His heart thumped.

After a long moment, Robbie shrugged. "Keep your hands to yourself and we'll get on fine, I reckon." He stopped by the horses, scratching one behind the ears. "Have to tie one to the wagon. I was expecting three men. What did 'em in?"

"Typhoid fever," Patrick answered. "Almost got me too."

"Truly? Someone must be lookin' out for you." He untied one of the horses and gave Patrick the reins. "Saddle up and enjoy it. I've seen some of the convict work crews out from time to time, and I daresay this is a better deal you two have gotten."

As Colin took his horse and swung himself into the saddle, he couldn't help but smile. He thought Robbie was quite right.

SEVERAL PAINFUL HOURS later, Colin was markedly less certain that he wouldn't rather be digging a ditch or doing anything else than ride a horse. Although he'd always loved riding at home, he'd never spent so many hours at a time on horseback. And after months at sea in cramped conditions and without proper food, he was weaker and thinner than he'd ever been.

Patrick seemed to be faring no better as the afternoon went on, although Colin knew he'd never admit it. Yet he could tell Patrick was just as weary as he was. The bout of typhoid still hadn't totally left him. At least the sun had mercifully disappeared behind a wall of clouds, and there was a breeze to cool them.

Added to their discomfort was the challenge of actually driving the cattle. Patrick was a skilled rider and accustomed to dealing with livestock, but Colin still heard him swear in frustration at errant cows. Robbie had conducted a rudimentary lesson that boiled down to: Keep the herd together and make them go where you want them to go.

Colin felt utterly out of his depth, and after a while, just staying on his horse was enough of a challenge. The road hadn't gone far, and the terrain was surprisingly rocky. Along with open spaces, there were swaths of forest. Robbie told them the land would get much hillier before it would flatten out as they continued.

The saddle Colin sat upon was unlike any he'd ever seen. It appeared to have been modified from a traditional English hunt saddle. Hunks of leather were sewn onto the sides and seemed to act as knee pads. The seat was much deeper and gave more stability than Colin was used to. Although he was exhausted, he felt secure on his horse's back.

His mount's name was Mission, and Colin scratched the horse's head and talked to him, trying to establish a rapport. Mission seemed friendly enough and was well trained. The cows, on the other hand, were a stubborn lot. Robbie had given them coiled whips, but Colin was reluctant to use his. He'd attached it to his belt and felt as if he was playing dress-up with William as they had as children.

Robbie had a real gun—a rifle that he kept with him in a scabbard by his saddlebag. Colin had never even touched a firearm. Hunting had never interested him. Still, considering the beasts that could be living out on this land, he was glad Robbie was armed.

As night fell, Robbie rode ahead to tell Emily to stop, and they drove the cattle into a clearing. Once the cattle were content to stay put and graze, Colin gratefully slid off his horse. Of course, he ended up all the way on the ground as his legs gave way beneath him. He took a deep breath and mustered up the will to stand, although he was quite content to stay on the ground for the moment. As he struggled to his knees, Patrick was suddenly there, his grip firm on Colin's arm as he helped him to his feet.

Colin smiled faintly. "Haven't gotten my land legs back yet."

Patrick's hand lingered. "You're doing fine."

Robbie approached, flipping his hat in his hand and catching it repeatedly. "All right, there?"

"Yes." Colin brushed off the seat of his trousers. "Thank you."

Robbie looked him up and down, then shouted to Emily by the wagon. "They'll need better boots, ma'am."

Emily approached, back ramrod straight as she attempted to smooth down her hair, which was coming loose from its knot. Her mourning dress was now covered in a fine layer of dust and dirt, and she appeared as exhausted as Colin felt. "Will there be suitable boots in the town we're nearing?"

"Yes, although it's more of a general store, ma'am. Not so much a town as you might imagine. It's on a property. One of the new cattle stations. *Bagaaybaraay*, it's called."

Colin, Patrick, and Emily all stared at Robbie as if he was speaking a foreign language, which he soon explained he was. Colin had known there were indigenous people in Australia and wondered if they were anything like the Indians of the stories about America.

"What's for supper?" Robbie asked.

Emily looked at Colin and Patrick before realizing Robbie was addressing her. "I'm not sure. I'm not much of a cook."

"You did buy rations for the journey in Sydney, didn't you, ma'am?"

"Yes, but my husband assured me the cooking would be taken care of."

"Well, on a bigger drive, we'd have a food wagon, but with just us, we'll have to cook for ourselves. I'm sure we can come up with something." He grinned affably.

Colin was so hungry he'd eat anything, especially if it was fresh. Robbie started a fire with an effortlessness that Colin admired and envied. He then cooked up a stew, and they sat around the fire as it bubbled in a pot. Robbie seemed to be the only one with any energy left, and he carried on the conversation single-handedly, telling them about his last cattle drive and his adventures with a sudden flood.

All conversation stopped when he served up the meal, and Colin couldn't recall anything ever tasting quite as delicious. They washed it down with some whiskey, which Colin had never liked but could imagine developing a taste for. He and Patrick devoured their portions, and Robbie chuckled. "Didn't seem to feed you too well, eh? That's the government for you." He then spoke to Emily. "How are you finding it?"

She finished chewing and swallowed before answering. "It's quite pleasant. Thank you."

"Just wait till I catch us a kangaroo. Then we'll feast."

"Kangaroo?" Patrick asked.

"Yep. Kind of like…it's hard to say, really. A little horse, but they hop on their back legs. Not really like a horse at all, actually. Not like anything you'd know, I don't think. Strong as hell and quick bastards too." He glanced at Emily. "Excuse my language, ma'am."

Emily's expression was unchanging. "It's all right." She wiped her mouth daintily with a handkerchief. "There are blankets for you men. I trust I don't have to warn you to stay away from the wagon."

All three shook their heads, and Robbie smiled mischievously. "I reckon that's why you ended up with these two for your prisoners, ain't it?"

Emily nodded stiffly. "Yes. I suppose it is."

"Well, you've nothin' to worry about from me, ma'am. I'd sooner cut off my own…you know, than disrespect a good woman."

"That's very comforting, Robert."

Robbie jerked a thumb at Colin and Patrick. "Are you wanting to tie them up?"

Emily seemed very uncomfortable with the notion. "I hadn't considered the matter. Do you think we should?"

Robbie pondered it for a moment. "Nah. If I keep the horses with me, I reckon it'll be fine. They'd be fools to run for it." He addressed Colin and Patrick. "Trust me, you won't get far, and the colony doesn't look fondly on fugitives. Not one bit."

"We won't run," Patrick replied.

"It really isn't necessary to bind us," Colin added. He had no idea where they'd run to in this unfamiliar land.

"Very well. Good night." Emily retreated to the wagon some yards away.

Robbie untied the horses from where they'd been left by a tree and took their reins. "You seem like decent enough fellas. But I warn you, I sleep with one eye open, and like I said, you wouldn't get far. I'd really rather you didn't give me any reason to dislike you."

"You've got nothing to worry about from us," Patrick answered.

"Right, then. I'll take watch tonight, over yonder on the other side of the herd. We'll take turns as we go along and you two get more familiar with the cattle. You just have to keep an ear out in case they get spooked by something. Don't want a stampede."

"No, I imagine we don't," Colin said.

"One of you do the washing up in the stream. Watch your step, though. Snakes come out at night."

"Snakes?" Colin and Patrick exclaimed in unison.

Robbie grinned. "Just pullin' your legs." Over his shoulder as he walked away, the horses in tow, he called back, "There are snakes, though. Day *and* night. So be careful."

Colin and Patrick looked at each other and couldn't help but laugh. "Can you believe we're here?" Colin waved his arm to encompass their surroundings. The stars shone impossibly bright, and the sky seemed massive. "Just this morning we were still on that damn ship."

"Indeed. It's an odd feeling. Like a dream."

Colin bent to collect the metal dishes. "Lucky thing, as it turns out. Being debauched. We might have ended up breaking rocks, wearing leg irons."

"Lucky indeed. If you can call being a prisoner for the crime of being ourselves lucky." Patrick's tone was resentful.

"True. But you know what I mean."

Patrick softened. "Aye. I know what you mean, Colin."

Colin's stomach flip-flopped at the sound of his name on Patrick's tongue. He took a step closer. "I'm so glad to be here with you. I don't know what I would have done—"

Patrick suddenly took the dishes from Colin's hands. "I'll do the washing. You'd best get to bed, Lord." He strode away into the darkness.

With a sigh, Colin collected their blankets from where Emily had left them outside the wagon. He spread them by the dying fire, making a bed for Patrick a respectable distance away. He lay down and listened for Patrick's return, but was fast asleep in no time at all.

WHEN COLIN WOKE, he experienced a few moments of dissonance. There was an unfamiliar low din he couldn't identify, and his bunk felt strange and unmoving beneath him. He wondered if the ship was so still because they'd stopped in port, which meant they'd have to stay on the prison deck.

However, as he opened his eyes, the dim barracks weren't there, and he breathed in clean, fresh air. Instead of rows of narrow bunks and snoring convicts, Colin took in a herd of lowing cattle. The events of the day before clicked into place in his mind, and he sat up to peer around, still disbelieving that he was really out in the Australian bush. Better yet, that he was with Patrick.

He'd slept like a rock all night. The sun had appeared just over the horizon, and he stretched his arms overhead as Patrick approached from the creek. Patrick took a swig from a canteen and stopped a yard away. "What're you so happy about this morning?"

"Happy to be off that ship. Happy to not be in a cell or on a road gang." Colin paused before finishing his thought. "Happy to be with you, whether you like it or not. Happy that Mrs. Grant seems a good woman, and Robbie is friendly and kind from what I can tell so far."

Patrick shook his head. "What did I tell you? *Don't trust anyone*. Look out for yourself, because no one else will."

Colin wanted to ask if they couldn't look out for each other, but held his tongue. Emily emerged from the wagon a few minutes later, clad again in the black dress. It was high necked and made of fairly thick material. Colin thought she would be quite uncomfortable wearing it in the heat, but supposed she felt duty bound.

Whistling a jaunty tune, Robbie returned with the horses. He started a fire and brewed a pot of strong coffee. They ate yesterday's stew, which tasted just as good to Colin as it had the night before. The coffee was bitter, but he forced it down.

The notion of spending the entire day in the saddle was daunting. Yet Colin had no choice, so he mounted Mission, squared his shoulders, and spurred his horse, trying to ignore the ache in his muscles. As they moved onward over stretches of fields and past trees, Robbie would ride ahead every so often to give Emily directions.

Late morning, they stopped to rest the cattle and horses, and Colin was quite grateful for the respite. Robbie pointed out some small trees that were growing clusters of round, pale green fruit.

"Desert limes, these are. If you're ever scarce of water, find some of these. Taste a bit strong, but they're food for ya."

They picked a few each, and Colin peeled the skin tentatively. His first bite was sharp but didn't taste too bad. They snacked on nuts as well, of which there seemed to be plenty growing on the land.

After eating, Robbie handed Colin and Patrick each a coil of rope. Patrick was already handy with a rope thanks to his work with horses, so Robbie showed Colin the best way to knot a loop in the end and then demonstrated spinning the rope above his head and tossing it neatly over a rock quite some distance away.

"Once you've got a feel for it, you can work on your aim. Of course, misbehavin' cows aren't likely to be standing as still as that rock is." Robbie grinned.

Colin's first attempt landed only a few feet away in a tangled heap, much to his embarrassment. Yet Robbie didn't mock him. "That was a good try. Don't worry, it takes some practice." He clapped Colin on the shoulder encouragingly.

Patrick's toss went much farther than Colin's but didn't quite make the target. Patrick's jaw set, and he yanked the rope back to try again. They each had a few more throws—with much more success on Patrick's part—and Robbie told them to keep the ropes so they could practice whenever they had a moment.

Back on their horses, Robbie effortlessly tossed his rope over the head of a nearby cow. Colin was determined to master the technique and asked Robbie to demonstrate again. He did, and then they were back on the trail.

The clouds of the day before were gone, and the sun was powerful. Colin knew his exposed skin was burning but, without a hat, couldn't do much about it. At least his arms and legs were covered. He hoped they'd reach the store sooner rather than later.

Midday, Colin got his first look at several kangaroos as they bounced across the land, jumping remarkably high and moving quickly. Patrick and Colin exchanged amazed grins as they watched the strange animals springing along on powerful back legs. Colin could hardly believe he was still on the same planet as England. Australia was an utterly foreign world.

That night, they set up camp over a rise from a still pond that had formed off a river. After the cows were settled, Robbie jerked his thumb in the pond's direction. "Ma'am, you get first crack at the billabong."

Emily brushed some dust from her forehead. "Pardon?"

"The billabong. That pond over yonder. That's what we call it. Don't know why, exactly." Although Robbie spoke with an accent that was largely plebian British, at times there was quite a twang to his dialect, and some of the words he used were fascinating to Colin.

"Oh, I see. *Billabong*." Emily seemed to enjoy rolling the word over her tongue.

"Like I said, ladies first. Don't worry; we can't see from here. We'll make tucker in the meantime."

While Emily bathed and Patrick rubbed down the horses, Colin and Robbie assembled a simple meal of dried meat and a soupy vegetable mixture. After being at sea, Colin was well and truly tired of dried meat and hoped Robbie would be able to hunt something fresh the next day.

Emily returned with her wet hair slicked back in a knot and her black dress on once more. Colin wondered if she was sleeping in it too. By the time Robbie had his turn and they ate, the sun was down. Patrick told Colin to take his bath first, and he and Robbie discussed who would take watch as Emily retired to her wagon, closing the canvas flaps tightly.

At the billabong's edge, Colin stripped off his clothes, which would need to be laundered very soon. Although he was quite conscious of the fact that there could be snakes or any other number of unknown creatures about, the lure of the cool water was far too enticing. He stepped in and pushed off, submerging.

The water was like a balm on his tired muscles and burned scalp, and he closed his eyes for a minute and floated peacefully. Although he would have been happy to stay there all night, Colin knew he couldn't. He realized he'd left the bar of soap on the shore and stood up and opened his eyes.

Patrick stood by the pile of Colin's discarded clothes, the soap in one of his large hands. In the moonlight, they watched each other silently. Colin's throat was dry, and his body hummed with desire.

Without a word, Patrick slowly peeled off his clothing, folding each piece carefully as Colin's excitement grew. When he was naked, his cock already springing to life, Patrick steadily waded in until they were face-to-face in the waist-high water. Colin leaned in to kiss him, but Patrick turned him about with deft hands, pulling him tightly against his chest.

Patrick dipped the bar of soap in the water in front of Colin and lathered his hands slowly. Just as Colin was about to beg him to hurry, Patrick caressed Colin's chest and arms, sucking on the juncture of Colin's shoulder and neck. Taking time to lather every so often, Patrick washed him, although maddeningly, he didn't touch Colin's groin.

Colin's cock was rock hard, but when he moved to touch it, Patrick tightened an arm around his chest. He sucked on Colin's earlobe, and his tongue teased the tender skin behind Colin's ear. One hand snaked down, and Patrick eased the tip of his finger into Colin's asshole.

Gasping at the sensation, Colin pushed back, wanting more. He felt as if his body was alight as Patrick slipped in farther, stroking lightly. Colin's breath came in short pants, and he moaned loudly when Patrick reached down with his other hand and fisted Colin's cock, rubbing and twisting.

Patrick slid in another finger and stretched Colin, who leaned against him, slack with pleasure as Patrick played him like a virtuoso would a violin. Colin moaned as the delicious tension built. He could imagine even better than before what it would be like to have Patrick inside him, and he pushed back, wanting more, feeling Patrick's hardness jutting into his lower back.

Crooking his fingers, Patrick rubbed against a spot that made Colin practically vibrate out of the water, gasping. He repeated the motion, and Colin came, shuddering against Patrick as the sensations overtook him. Patrick squeezed and milked Colin's cock until it was too sensitive to touch and Colin turned in his arms.

There was an affectionate twinkle in Patrick's eye. Colin wanted to kiss him so much, but instead reached down and stroked him. Patrick's eyes drifted shut, and he leaned into Colin's touch. Suddenly a shriek erupted in the night, and they both jumped.

They stared at each other for a moment, and then Patrick groaned in frustration and moved toward shore. They both tugged on their trousers quickly and ran over the rise to camp to find Emily by the wagon in a white, long-sleeved nightdress that grazed her ankles. Her thick hair hung loose down her back.

A lantern wobbled inside the wagon, and Robbie's voice rang out. "Don't see anything, ma'am."

Emily's arms were folded tightly around herself. "I swear I felt something crawling on my leg."

Robbie emerged. "I believe you. But I can't find it now, and there's a good chance you scared it to death by screaming like that." He smiled, obviously trying to lighten her mood, but she remained coiled and tense.

"Thank you for looking." She brushed by him and back into the wagon, pulling the canvas shut after her.

Robbie leaned close to Colin and Patrick and whispered, "Could've been a redback, but we won't tell her that."

"What's that?" Colin whispered back, even though he was sure he didn't want to know the answer.

They moved away from the wagon, and Robbie answered. "Just a wee little spider, but it'll kill a grown man. It's black with a red stripe. If you see one, don't try to pick it up."

Colin couldn't imagine a circumstance when he'd willingly pick up any spiders, let alone a poisonous one. "I'll remember that, thank you."

Patrick had disappeared back to the pond, and Colin supposed he couldn't very well go after him, although most of his clothes were still there. "Who's on watch tonight, then?" he asked.

Robbie rolled out his blanket near the remains of the fire, the horses tethered nearby. "Patrick said he'll take it. You can go tomorrow night. So get a good night's sleep tonight."

As Colin prepared his sleeping area, Patrick returned and silently deposited Colin's remaining clothing beside him. He brushed Colin's shoulder with his fingertips, and went to take his post.

Chapter Nine

WHEN COLIN HAULED himself into the saddle the next morning, he had to bite his lip to stop from gasping at the discomfort in his thighs and backside. He hoped as the days went on, his body would become accustomed to being on horseback for so many hours.

He could also feel a slight tenderness inside him where Patrick's fingers had explored, and a little thrill ran up his spine as he remembered. He wondered how it would feel after having Patrick's cock inside him, and he had to stop that train of thought as his trousers tightened.

A few hours into their travels, Colin noticed some cattle near the horizon. He rode up to Robbie. "Whose cows are those?"

"Owner's name is Jackson. We're on his station. Hasn't finished the fence yet."

"Really? This is all his land?"

Robbie chuckled. "Been on his land since yesterday."

Colin couldn't conceive of owning so much property. "And he doesn't mind?"

"As long as we don't poach his herd, nah. He owns the store, and your Mrs. Grant will be shelling out."

"Will we be there soon?"

"Not long now."

Colin hoped Robbie's idea of "not long" was the same as his.

As they rode on, he noticed a dog watching their progress from atop a boulder. "What's he doing out here all alone?"

Robbie followed Colin's gaze. "Wild dog. Dingoes, we call 'em."

"Are they dangerous?" It looked not unlike dogs Colin had encountered in England.

"Can be. Gotta watch your sheep and chickens if dingoes are about, that's for sure. But they're pets to some folks. If they're raised with people, they can be just like any other dog. Depends, I suppose."

Colin watched the animal with interest. He spotted a few more in the distance, but the dingoes didn't seem interested in approaching. On the other side of a rise, Colin could see two one-story buildings in the distance. It was the first sign of civilization since they had left Sydney, and Colin welcomed it gratefully.

The simple, clean general store was operated by a man and woman, both very dark-skinned and with broad features. Colin tried not to stare, and he noticed Patrick and Emily also sneaking glances. Coming from rural England and Ireland, they'd never seen anyone who wasn't Caucasian.

Emily instructed the couple to outfit Colin and Patrick with everything they needed to be stockmen. Soon they each had several pairs of rugged canvas trousers and long-sleeved shirts, along with various undershirts and garments. They were each given brown leather hats with wide brims in a roundish shape and long, matching coats, along with sturdy boots.

As Robbie put in an order for food supplies, Colin found himself by a shelf that held paper and ink supplies. He fingered one of the sheets longingly.

"Did you want some paper?" Emily stood behind him.

"Oh, I was just looking." Colin felt as if he'd been caught doing something wrong for some strange reason. "Although I would like to write my cousin and sister. I'm not sure how the mail works here, but I assume they have a system."

She looked at him for a long moment, her expression strange. "Yes, I assume they do. Pick out whatever you need."

"Thank you, Mrs. Grant." Colin smiled, and Emily nodded in reply and turned away.

Colin was sorry to say good-bye to the little outpost, but soon they were back on their way, driving the herd ever onward.

That night after dinner, Robbie stared up at the sky. Colin had noticed him doing the same the night before. He approached and cleared this throat. "Admirer of the constellations?"

"You could say that. They keep us on the right path, straight and true."

"You use them for navigation?"

"That's right. I've never been as far as we're headed, so the stars have to guide us."

Colin gazed up. The night sky was different on this side of the world, and out in the wild, the stars seemed to blaze far more brightly than they did in England somehow. "A thousand miles. I can't believe we're going that far." A thought occurred to Colin. "What will be waiting for us?"

"Mr. Grant commissioned a big house and some outbuildings. Hope they're built by the time we get there."

"Big house?"

"Where the owner and his family lives."

"And a station is like a farm."

Robbie chuckled. "I suppose. A very, very large farm. Some are thousands of square miles."

Colin thought of his home in England and how proud his parents were of their few acres. "I can't imagine owning that much land."

"Well, the likes of us likely won't have to worry about that. I'll spend my life working for the landowners. You might too, if you're lucky. Get a ticket-of-leave so you can work and travel around. Maybe even a certificate of freedom if you play your cards right."

"I didn't know such things existed. How do you earn them?"

"Just mind yourself and be a model prisoner, I reckon." Robbie returned Colin's smile. "So far I'd say you're doing well."

Colin thought about the possibility of earning his freedom the rest of the day and eagerly told Patrick after dinner. Patrick listened carefully but was less optimistic. "We'll see. You can't get your hopes up. Remember, we've been here less than a week. Still plenty of sentence to serve first."

Although he knew Patrick was right, Colin couldn't help but remain hopeful that one day he'd be a free man again. Yet when he thought about what exactly he might do as a free man, he was less sure.

That night, Colin took the watch. He leaned against a tree on the far side of the herd and dozed fitfully, waking up at the slightest sound. Although he knew snakes and wild creatures could certainly attack when he slept in camp, out by himself, his imagination ran wild.

Fortunately, he emerged from his watch unscathed, and they moved northward with the cattle. They quickly settled into a comfortable rhythm as the days turned into weeks. Driving the cattle was hard work for all, and Colin often fell asleep after barely finishing his supper.

Emily—still clad in her mourning dress day in, day out—kept to herself and only spoke when necessary. She had begun cooking more of their meals, with varying success. Robbie was always quick to compliment her and at times tried to coax her into conversation, to little avail.

Colin enjoyed Robbie's company very much, and he was sure Patrick did as well. The trio worked well together, and Robbie was a patient instructor. Colin practiced his roping every chance he got and had begun to snag rocks and bushes. He wasn't sure how he'd manage on a moving horse, but he was improving.

Whenever they could, Colin and Patrick came together furtively as they had on the ship—giving each other release with hands and mouths. Colin longed to truly lie with Patrick, to be with him and not have to constantly look over their shoulders for fear of being discovered. Colin wasn't sure what would happen if Robbie or Emily caught them. They were already prisoners, after all. Yet he knew a much worse fate might await them if they were found out.

After a month on the drive, Colin felt more at ease in the saddle than he had ever expected. Robbie was a talented hunter, and they ate a steady supply of game—kangaroo, wallaby (which to Colin's eyes was simply a smaller kangaroo), and large birds. Colin had regained his strength after the voyage and then some.

From time to time, they came across tribes of Aborigines. The natives regarded them with open curiosity and did not appear hostile, which was a relief. They kept their distance but followed along at times for miles.

Wearing little to cover themselves, Colin imagined their bare feet must be hard as stones on the bottom to travel over the hot earth and rough land. He wondered what they must think of him and his companions and the large beasts they herded. How strange it must be to have foreigners arrive on your shores, unexpected and uninvited.

Colin wrote long letters to William detailing the things he'd seen and done, along with several to Rebecca. Even once to his parents, although it had been short. Colin wasn't sure when he'd actually be able to mail them, but when he had the time, he enjoyed recording his activities. He could hardly believe how different his life had become.

AFTER TRAVERSING COUNTRYSIDE that was relatively flat, they eventually encountered terrain that was a great deal hillier. It was a struggle for the cattle and horses to conquer some of the rises, and inconveniently placed trees added to their exertion.

As the cattle stubbornly came to a halt on one such hill on a sunny October afternoon, Robbie instructed Colin to ride ahead and see what was blocking them. Colin stood in the saddle as Mission picked his way up the steep slope. A hundred feet from the crest of the hill, Colin spotted the wagon. It appeared stuck on a rock, and Emily had her shoulder into the wooden vehicle, trying to dislodge it.

Colin urged Mission on faster and called out to her. "Mrs. Grant! Wait, let me help you."

Emily either couldn't hear or ignored him, as she still strained to free the wagon wheel from the rock it was caught on. Colin dismounted and tied Mission to a nearby tree. "Mrs. Grant, I can do that."

"No!" Emily swiped at her hair, which spilled from its knot. Her face was alarmingly flushed. "I don't need your help. I don't need anyone's help."

Colin stayed a few feet away. He'd never seen her so on edge. "Why don't you drink some water and rest for a moment?"

She shook her head and shoved at the wagon again. Her mourning dress was filthy, and Colin could imagine how sweltering it was with the merciless sun overhead. Her hat was nowhere to be seen. Colin took a step closer. "Please, Mrs. Grant. I'm here to help you, after all."

Emily spun around and slammed her fists into Colin's chest with surprising force, shoving him back. "You're here because that son of a bitch left me alone!" Her shoulders shook, tears spilling down her cheeks. "This was *his* dream! I was happy in England! We had a good life! Now what do I have?" She threw her arm out and waved it around. "*This?*"

"I-I'm sorry." Emily was always so guarded, and Colin was at a loss seeing her undone. He cast about for something else to say. "I remember seeing you with your husband on the ship one day."

This caught her attention. "You did?" She wiped her cheeks, yet the tears fell unabated.

"Yes. He was making you laugh."

Of course, it only served to increase her sobs. Colin watched helplessly for a moment and then reached out a tentative hand and drew her close. After momentary resistance, she collapsed against him, head on his chest as he wrapped his arms around her. Her legs gave out, and they sank to the ground as she wailed her anger and grief.

The sound must have traveled downhill, as Robbie and Patrick thundered up a few minutes later. They dismounted and stopped a few yards away, eyes wide. As Emily's sobs abated, Patrick passed Colin a canteen, and Colin encouraged her to drink. Robbie handed her a handkerchief, and for the first time since that long-ago day on the ship, Colin saw her smile.

It faded, and fresh guilt and grief welled up and overflowed, and Colin held her for a while longer while Robbie and Patrick set about getting the wagon free. Once they did, Robbie cleared his throat. "We have to get moving, ma'am. I'm sorry, but we must."

Sniffling, Emily extricated herself from Colin's arms. "Yes, of course. I apologize for my…outburst."

The three men awkwardly assured her it was naught, and Colin retrieved Mission as Patrick and Robbie headed back downhill. Seated in the driver's seat of the wagon again, Emily blew her nose into the handkerchief.

"Just shout if the wagon gets stuck again, Mrs. Grant. Or for anything, if you need to." Colin wheeled Mission around.

"Colin."

He looked back over his shoulder and pulled on the reins. It was the first time Emily had called him by name. Or by anything.

"Thank you."

"You're welcome."

"You're not at all what I expected, you know."

"What did you expect?"

"I don't know, honestly. Not a Cambridge man, that's certain."

Colin smiled. "Didn't quite make it to Cambridge, I'm afraid."

"Lucky for me, Colin. It's a comfort, having an English gentleman about. You're very decent and kind."

Colin felt a warmth in his chest. He found Emily's opinion meant a great deal to him. "Thank you, Mrs. Grant. If you ever need to talk, I'm happy to listen."

"Thank you."

Giving Mission a nudge with his heels, Colin headed back to the herd, and they carried on. Although he knew he was a prisoner and she his captor, it certainly didn't feel like it. He would like very much to have a new friend.

THE NEXT MORNING when she emerged from the wagon, Emily wore a light blue summer dress of thin material. Robbie simply stared, and Patrick tipped his hat. "You look well this morning, Mrs. Grant."

"Thank you, Patrick."

Colin wished her good morning, and she smiled back tentatively. He hoped this day would mark a new beginning for her.

They continued over hilly country for several more days, coming to rest one night on a flat plateau below a rocky peak. The sun hadn't set yet, but Robbie had determined the rest of the hill too uneven for the cattle and they'd have to go the long away around.

Pleased to be stopping a bit early for the day, Colin hiked up the rest of the way to watch the sunset. He clambered over and between large rocks, and by the time he was at the top, he couldn't see the camp behind him, as it was hidden behind the boulders. The only thing visible in all directions was the landscape—a foreign terrain of rocky hills, groups of trees, dry grass and shrubs, and flat, red earth in the very distance.

As the sun sank, the air cooled remarkably. Colin ran his hand through his growing hair and looked out over the land peacefully. Someone approached, and he turned to see Patrick stop a few feet away.

Colin smiled. "Isn't it remarkable?"

"Which aspect in particular?" Patrick's tone was light.

"All of it. Look at where we're standing. It's incredible. Being here. Before you say it, I know we're prisoners. But I've never felt so…at peace."

"Aye, it suits you, this life."

"Who would have thought when you were teaching me to ride all those years ago that we'd end up here?"

"Certainly not me when you were running around underfoot."

Colin chuckled. "My father hated it when I spent all that time with you. I loved it, though."

"So why'd you stop?" Patrick picked up a stone and tossed it over the edge. "You grew up and had better things to do? It puzzled me."

Colin weighed whether or not he should tell the truth and figured there was no harm any longer. "You're going to laugh when I tell you, I bet. You remember that groundskeeper? He was only around a year or so. I don't recall his name."

Patrick pondered it for a moment. "Oh, him." His brow furrowed. "What about him?"

"I saw you with him one day in the stable. It was pouring rain, a great storm. I hid and watched, and afterward I was so ashamed of the desire I felt. It was…very confusing at the time. It seems forever ago now. I couldn't dream of looking you in the eye after what I saw, so I stayed away."

Patrick stared with an unreadable expression and said nothing.

Colin laughed, disbelieving. "You're not angry, are you? I know it was wrong to spy, but I couldn't help myself." He smiled ruefully. "I wished it was me you were with. Still do, I suppose."

For a long moment, their eyes met. Then in two strides, Patrick had Colin's head in his hands, and he kissed him long and hard, plunging his tongue into Colin's mouth. After a moment of surprise, Colin kissed him back, shivering with sudden desire as he pulled Patrick closer.

Colin's head spun as they panted for breath and kissed each other again, tongues invading and exploring. It was the first *real* kiss he'd ever had, and Colin's body was absolutely alight. They rubbed against each other, hands everywhere as they kissed with a desperation that had sparked and spread like wildfire.

It was as if a floodgate had opened. Colin wrapped his arms around Patrick's back, wanting him closer, closer. Patrick kissed him senseless, doing things with his tongue that Colin hadn't known possible.

"Supper!" Robbie's shout echoed up.

They tore apart and caught their breath, foreheads pressed together. Colin knew they had to return to camp, but he sought Patrick's mouth again anyway, hungry for more. *To the devil with supper.* Patrick cupped Colin's face in his hand, kissing him deeply. There was another shout, and they groaned in unison, unwilling to stop.

Patrick drew back and gazed at Colin with an expression so tender, it stopped the breath in Colin's chest. He pressed a last kiss to Colin's lips and stepped back. Reluctantly, they straightened their clothing. Colin wanted nothing more than to shuck all his garments at once and mate with Patrick on the dusty ground. Yet he knew they mustn't.

They took their time walking back down to camp. By the time they arrived, their erections had subsided, at least. Robbie gave Colin a strange look but said nothing. They ate in silence aside from the odd comment to compliment Emily on the stew, which was truly much improved.

Colin was consumed with thoughts of what had just happened. Patrick had never kissed him before, not truly. It had felt intimate in a way that even pleasuring each other with their mouths hadn't. He wasn't sure how to describe it, but he knew he wanted more. Much, much more.

First he had to suffer through their usual nightly routine. There was no river or stream nearby, so Patrick rinsed the dishes with a small amount of drinking water and stored them in the food crate in the wagon. It had only rained a few times since they'd been on the drive, and with summer upon them, water would be more and more scarce. But for now, they had more than enough.

Emily said good night, and Robbie laid out his canvas bedroll, falling asleep in minutes. It was Patrick's turn on watch, and he left with his canteen and small pack with snacks if he needed to stay awake. He said nothing to Colin and didn't even meet his gaze.

After arranging his own bedroll, Colin stretched out and stared up at the night sky, his heart beating rapidly. He hoped Patrick was waiting for him, wanting to kiss him again. Wanting to kiss him forever.

Yet perhaps Patrick regretted it. Colin's mind raced. He desperately wanted more, and the connection between them had been incredibly intense. Or so he thought—what if it was just in his own mind?

The only sound in the night was of crickets and Robbie's snores, along with the odd shuffling or mooing from the herd. Colin usually had no trouble sleeping after their long days, but tonight he knew sleep wouldn't come.

He waited almost an hour before coming to his decision. Creeping slowly, bedroll in hand, he skirted around the herd, careful not to disturb any of the cattle. Patrick leaned against a tree on the far side. He appeared to be sleeping, but as Colin knelt before him, Patrick opened his eyes. "I didn't think you were coming," he whispered.

Colin kissed him in response, yanking at Patrick's stubborn clothing. Patrick laughed softly and unbuttoned Colin's shirt. He was moving far too slowly for Colin's liking, and Colin squirmed away, tugging down his own trousers as he pulled Patrick onto the bedroll. Colin got on his hands and knees.

He waited for Patrick to enter him, but instead, Patrick stole a hand below his shirt and caressed his spine. He kissed the back of Colin's neck. "Shh. Slowly."

"No, please. *Please*, Patrick." Colin didn't think he could wait another moment without exploding.

With gentle hands, Patrick urged him onto his back and straddled him. Patrick's shirt hung half-open and his trousers were still buttoned, so Colin reached for the fastenings. Patrick caught his wrists and leaned down to kiss him. "Relax."

Colin shook his head, and Patrick kissed him again. "I don't want to hurt you."

"I don't care."

In the moonlight, Patrick gazed down intently, brushing Colin's growing hair back from his forehead. "I do."

Patrick pressed their lips together, kissing Colin leisurely. Although he was consumed with the desire to finally lie with Patrick properly, Patrick seemed set on not rushing as he explored Colin's mouth. Finally Patrick reached for his small satchel. He took out a metal tin and placed it on the ground beside them. Colin was about to ask what it was, but Patrick's tongue slipped inside his mouth once more. With nimble fingers, Patrick removed the remnants of Colin's clothing and then his own.

He stretched out over Colin languidly, his lips traveling over Colin's skin, teasing and caressing. He took one of Colin's nipples into his mouth, sucking gently, swirling his tongue around the sensitive flesh. His fingers drifted down to the soft skin of Colin's belly, skimming lightly, dipping lower through the thatch of hair but somehow not touching Colin's cock, which jutted out, hard and leaking.

As Patrick shifted his attention over to the neglected nipple, Colin moaned. "Please. Hurry."

Patrick ignored him and continued the delicious torture. His mouth traveled southward, and he dipped his tongue into the indent in Colin's stomach. Patrick's fingers were light on Colin's inner thighs, the faint touch unbearable, stoking the fires of his already blazing desire. He tingled from head to toe, and he needed more.

Finally, Patrick relented and straddled Colin once more. He removed the lid and held the tin out for Colin. "Cooking grease. Dip your fingers in." Colin did as instructed, the thick, viscous oil slick on his skin. Colin smeared the grease over Patrick's thick, throbbing cock, coating the silky hardness. Patrick pulsed in Colin's grasp, and Colin's mouth went dry with anticipation.

Shifting back, Patrick bent Colin's legs until his feet were flat on the blanket. He scooped some more grease with two of his fingers and slowly penetrated Colin's hole. First with one finger and then two, Patrick stretched him with measured movements, coating him with the slippery grease.

Colin thought he might spill from that alone and squeezed the base of his cock to calm himself as Patrick slipped his fingers out. Patrick pressed one of Colin's knees back toward his chest and urged him to wrap his other leg around Patrick's waist. Colin was open and exposed and very, very excited.

"Breathe," Patrick whispered as he moved closer, the head of his cock pressing at Colin's opening.

Taking in a shuddering breath, Colin willed himself to relax as Patrick inched inside. It burned, and Colin's eyes watered despite himself. Patrick stopped moving, holding still above Colin on his powerful arms. When the pain lessened, Colin urged him on, digging his fingers into Patrick's lower back.

The sting as Patrick eased into him was mixed with flares of sheer pleasure. Patrick pulled back a few inches and pushed in farther, and Colin gasped as his softening cock twitched back to life.

With infinite patience, Patrick worked all the way inside. Colin could feel Patrick's bollocks against his ass, and even in the darkness, he could see they were fully joined. He had never felt so full. So *complete*.

Tears prickled again, and Patrick leaned down to press tender kisses to Colin's eyelids and cheeks. They kissed, tongues winding together as Colin adjusted to the extraordinary sensation of Patrick inside him. He squeezed experimentally with his inner muscles, and Patrick encouraged him. "That's it."

After sliding out several inches, Patrick rocked back in, and Colin moaned. He swore he could see sparks before his eyes as Patrick moved inside him, the burning rub exquisite. Even with the gentle night breeze, sweat beaded on their skin, sticky with the remnants of the grease as their hands caressed.

Patrick took hold of Colin's leaking cock, stroking it in time with the thrusts of his hips. The lingering pain fused with the pleasure, and Colin had to bite his lip to keep from crying out in ecstasy as Patrick filled him. It was better than he'd ever imagined, and his cock tingled as the pressure built inexorably.

After a few more strokes, Colin spilled onto his chest in long, ropy threads as the fiery pleasure erupted. Patrick had to clap his hand over Colin's mouth to stifle his cries as Colin shuddered, eyes closed as he experienced a surge of bliss in every pore. With only a few more pumps of his hips and a low groan, Patrick came, hot and wet, deep inside Colin.

Patrick still held his weight on his arms, which trembled slightly as he took a deep breath. He pressed a kiss to the tip of Colin's nose and pulled out slowly, seeming to take great care. Colin winced and felt a strange emptiness. Patrick stretched out beside him, snaking his arm around Colin's shoulders. Colin laid his head on Patrick's chest, utterly content. He could hear Patrick's heartbeat slow down to normal, and he caressed Patrick's stomach with his fingertips.

The breeze rustled the leaves overhead, and the cattle nearby made low sounds from time to time. Colin knew he had to go back to camp, that he couldn't spend the night in Patrick's arms, as much as he wanted to. He longed for the day they could lie together in a bed. *Their* bed.

"You should go back." Patrick's voice was sleepy and sated. He traced an unknown pattern on Colin's back with his fingertips.

"I know. Just a few more minutes."

Patrick stroked Colin's hair and pressed a kiss to the top of his head. He didn't argue.

Chapter Ten

BEFORE COLIN OPENED his eyes the next morning, he took a minute to remember what it had been like to finally be with Patrick completely. As he relived it in his mind, his morning hardness strained against his trousers, longing to be touched.

He could hear the sounds of Emily stirring, so Colin quickly got up and ducked into a thick stand of trees nearby. Taking himself in hand, he leaned against the smooth trunk of a gum tree and brought himself to completion, eyes closed as he remembered the feel of Patrick moving inside him.

Colin's ass was tender, but the soreness delighted him. He supposed it was silly, but he felt as if he was a true man now. That he'd crossed a threshold in his mind by the actions of his body.

When Patrick arrived back at camp, Colin bid him good morning as usual and watched him closely, waiting for…something. However, to Patrick it was evidently a day like any other. He grunted a greeting to Colin, Robbie, and Emily and silently drank a steaming cup of coffee.

Colin's heart sank. Perhaps what they'd shared hadn't meant anything to Patrick after all. Yet he'd been so tender. Loving, even. When he'd kissed Colin on the hilltop—*really* kissed him—Colin was sure he'd felt a surrender between them. To say nothing of what had come later.

But in the morning's light, Patrick didn't seem the slightest bit affected. The four of them packed up as usual, and Colin tried to act like nothing was wrong. He failed, evidently. As he tightened the saddle on Mission, Emily approached.

She peered at him for a moment. "Are you feeling well this morning?"

Colin attempted a pleasant expression. "Yes, fine. Thank you."

Emily seemed unconvinced but didn't press. Colin mounted his horse and winced as he settled down on his backside. It would be a very long day. He squirmed, trying to find a comfortable angle. Looking up, he found Patrick watching from his horse some yards away. Patrick's lips twitched into a secret smile, and Colin's heart skipped a beat. He found himself smiling back, and suddenly it seemed as if the day wouldn't be so bad after all.

Although his ass ached even more by the time they stopped for lunch, Colin's good spirits remained. That morning, they had made their way around the rocky hill and moved across rolling land peppered with forests. As they traveled northwest, it became drier, the earth redder.

They stopped by a stream to rest the animals, and Robbie disappeared into the woods to hunt game for supper. Emily dished out remainders from the stew the night before, along with some nuts and plum-like fruit she'd picked the day before. She took her lunch and sat against a tree with a book. She wore a yellow dress that set off the gold in her hair perfectly, and seemed quite content. Colin was very glad to see her in better spirits.

After eating silently, Patrick caught Colin's gaze and gave a little nod of his head toward the stream. Colin followed him down the sloping embankment. With a last glance over his shoulder, Patrick knelt on the grass by the edge of the water. Colin did the same and realized they were low enough below the gentle slope that Emily couldn't see them if she happened to look up from her book.

Patrick patted Colin's bottom playfully. "How are you feeling today, Lord?"

Colin grumbled about the hated nickname. "Feels as though you'll never get another crack if you don't stop calling me that."

Patrick laughed and drew him close for a kiss, caressing Colin's buttocks lightly. There was no fire or hurry in their touch, but a sweetness that Colin drank in like honey. He explored Patrick's mouth with his tongue, lightly sweeping over his teeth and stroking Patrick's tongue.

Too soon, they heard a gunshot signaling Robbie's imminent return with supper in hand, and broke apart reluctantly. The day continued in a familiar routine, and Colin eagerly anticipated nightfall and the chance to perhaps be alone with Patrick again.

The first sign of trouble was a sound of distress that jolted Colin from his reverie. The noise was followed by another low call of terror from one of the cattle, and then drowned out by a thunder of hooves so loud Colin could feel the vibrations in his bones.

He hadn't known cattle could move so quickly, but they roared across the land. He could see Robbie gallop ahead to try and steer them away from Emily and the wagon. Colin wasn't sure what to do, and he spurred Mission on, his heart pounding.

In the distance rose a steep, jagged hill, and Colin realized Robbie was trying to angle the herd toward it. Patrick rode up alongside Colin, and without a word, they joined Robbie and pulled out their whips, driving the cattle closer to the rocky barrier.

Colin hated using the whip but knew it was for the animals' own good. Robbie had told him that stampeding cows were known to careen off cliffs or break their legs on uneven terrain. Gripping the reins with his left hand, Colin galloped alongside the stampeding herd. The din was overwhelming, and his breath came in short pants as his whip cracked through the air. Excitement and fear mingled, coursing through him.

The hill loomed closer, and to his immense relief, the cattle in the lead slid to a halt, forcing the others to follow suit. They mooed stridently, stepping to and fro, restless and keyed up. But they stayed put for the most part and seemed largely uninjured. Colin took a deep breath and blew it out, relieved.

Just then, a younger cow darted away from the pack, and Colin wheeled about, his pulse racing anew. In pursuit, he reached for his rope and swung it over his head with his right arm.

His first toss landed uselessly on the cow's rump. Colin cursed and yanked the rope back to try again. His second attempt missed the cow's head by inches, and Colin dug his heels into Mission's flanks to spur him on that much faster.

Colin swung the rope for a third time. His breath lodged in his throat as the rope sailed out, uncoiling in the air, seemingly suspended in time. Then it landed perfectly over the cow's head. A cry of victory erupted from him, and he tugged the rope and brought Mission to a stop.

His chest rising and falling with the exertion and excitement, Colin lifted his hat to wipe the sweat from his forehead. He drew the cow near and reached down to pat it gently, hoping to calm it. When the animal seemed less skittish, Colin trotted back to the herd with it in tow.

As he approached, Robbie tipped his hat. "Well done!"

"Thank you." Colin glowed with pride. He felt strong and capable in a way that was new to him. Patrick was tending to a cow a short distance away from the herd. Cattle shuffled discontentedly from time to time, but overall the animals were much calmer. Colin rode over to Patrick, who was stroking the injured cow soothingly as he gently poked and prodded. "Is it hurt?"

Patrick glanced up from examining one of the animal's bloody legs. "A bit cut and bruised, but she should be fine. Tracked down the runaway, eh?"

Colin grinned. "Yes. Roped it and all. Never thought I'd be

able to do it."

"When you put your mind to something, it seems you're capable of many things, Lord." Patrick winked.

The wagon rumbled up, and Emily jumped down, her face etched in concern. "Is everyone all right?"

Robbie took off his hat and began fiddling with it, flipping it around with one hand. "Yes, ma'am. How're you faring?"

She tucked an errant hair behind her ear. "Fine, fine. What on earth happened to startle them so?"

Robbie shrugged. "One of them got spooked by something. Might have been a snake or some other nasty critter. Hard to say, but once they get riled up, it's hard to stop 'em."

Emily looked at all three of them with admiration. "Well, you all handled it quite ably. Thank you."

"Hope you weren't too frightened, ma'am." Robbie spun his hat back onto his head.

"No. I knew you'd come through. After all, you're the best, are you not?" She smiled as she quoted his boast from the first day.

Robbie kicked a rock with the toe of his worn boot, and Colin could swear he was blushing. Robbie cleared his throat. "We'll stay here for the night. Let 'em get a good night's rest. It'll be a boon for all of us, I reckon."

Colin volunteered to accompany Robbie to the closest water source, a creek a couple of miles back. They cantered over a flat plain, and Colin enjoyed riding without having to mind the herd. As they neared the stream, they slowed their horses to a walk.

"You've taken to the saddle like a duck to water. Reckon you'll make a fine stockman," Robbie said.

"You really think so?" Colin beamed. He liked Robbie very much and found his approval meant a great deal.

"Truly." After a moment, he went on. "The way I see it, you don't deserve to be a prisoner. I've met plenty in my time, and you're not like any of 'em. Even my mum's a rougher sort than you." He chuckled.

Perplexed, Colin asked, "Your mother?"

"Came over on a ship about...well, I'm twenty-one, so it would have been twenty-two years ago or so."

"She was a *convict*?"

Robbie seemed blithely unconcerned. "Oh yeah. A woman of 'loose morals,' they called her. She did what she needed to survive. Her parents died when she was sixteen, and then she was on 'er own."

"How old was she when she was brought here?"

Robbie pondered for a moment. "Twenty-three. My dad picked her out of a line, and they were married not too long after."

"He picked her?"

"Not enough women here in the colony, so if a ship comes with any female prisoners, they dress 'em up and parade 'em out so the government officials can take their pick. If they ain't pretty enough, they get sent to the female factories. Do the laundry and other womanly tasks."

Colin had never considered that female prisoners were sent to the colony, as there had been none on his ship. "And if they're chosen by an official, are they released from serving their sentences?"

"If they marry. My mum got hitched to my dad right quick and had me so she could get her walking papers. Some of the officials use the women as whores an' never marry 'em. When they're used up, it's back to the factories."

"Are they happy? Your parents?"

They reached the water, and Robbie hopped off his horse and shrugged. "Get along fine, I suppose. She keeps the house and takes care of the rest of the kids. Got two brothers and a sister. I left home when I was fifteen to start work with the cattle. Don't see them but a few times a year, if that."

Colin slid off Mission's back and gave him a pat. "It doesn't bother anyone? That she was a convict?"

"Nah. Like I said, not enough women here. Can't be choosy."

"Too bad I'm not a woman, then," Colin joked.

Robbie laughed. "But then you wouldn't be out here chasing down runaway cattle. Darn sight more exciting, I reckon."

"That it is." Colin grew serious. "And it truly doesn't bother you? What I am? *Who* I am?"

Robbie knelt by the water and filled a container. "Thought it might at first, but you're both good blokes. Hard workers. Dependable. Out here you've got to rely on each other. Without your mates, you're done for."

"Mates." Colin liked the sound of that. He joined Robbie at the water's edge and filled one of their canteens.

"That's right. And honestly, you don't seem any different from the rest of us folks. Not that I see the appeal in it myself. Women are just…" His expression grew almost comically moony. "They're the best of God's creatures, from what I can tell."

"Any woman in particular?"

"Nah. Like I said, hard to find many here."

Emily came to mind, but Colin said nothing. "I'm sure you'll find a wonderful wife someday."

"You think?" Robbie grinned, pleased. "Well, I certainly don't have to worry about you or Patrick looking sideways in the meantime."

"No! Of course not. We wouldn't." Colin flushed.

Laughing, Robbie filled another container. "I know. You two only have eyes for each other."

"I…p-pardon? That's not… W-what I mean is, you're imagining things," Colin stammered.

"Right. If you say so." He shook his head, smiling. "You're mad for each other."

Colin knew he should argue. Buggery was no more legal in the colony than it was in England. But out in the wild, an eternity from civilization, it seemed silly to lie. "You really think so? About Patrick, I mean."

"It's plain as day." Robbie clapped Colin on the shoulder and went about filling the rest of his containers. Colin filled his, and they worked companionably. Robbie whistled a jolly tune, and even though he didn't quite know the song, Colin joined in anyway.

TWO DAYS LATER, Colin noticed the land had begun to flatten out and grow drier, the earth a more pronounced shade of red. There were still some hills and greenery, but it was less lush as they moved farther inland.

As they drove the herd across a large plain, clouds of dust appeared in the distance. Robbie seemed troubled. "Riders."

Sure enough, a group of men on horseback soon came into focus and were headed toward them. Emily stopped the wagon, and after Colin, Robbie, and Patrick settled the herd, they rode up to where Emily waited. The riders hadn't arrived yet, but would in less than a minute, Colin imagined.

"Who do you think they are?" Emily stood by the wagon, and Colin noted a rifle on her seat. He hadn't known she owned a weapon.

"Do you think they might be from the government? Coming to check on me and Patrick?" Colin asked.

Robbie gave him a strange look. "Check on you? Out here? Don't think so."

"But that was the arrangement, wasn't it?" Patrick spoke up. "Although it does seem unlikely given the size of this land. Can't quite imagine the breadth of it until you see for yourself."

"I'm sure it won't be until we're situated on the station," Emily said dismissively.

"But—"

Emily cut Robbie off. "Back to the matter at hand. Who do you think these men are?"

"Reckon it's Matthew Barnes. He was the first landowner to come this far northwest. Your husband secured the land past Barnes'. Don't fancy he's too happy about that, ma'am."

Colin and Patrick exchanged a wary glance. Emily gazed out at the riders. "Do you think they mean us harm?"

Robbie weighed his words carefully. "Probably not. We're on his land, so I expect they're coming to warn us off poaching from his herd. Let us know they're watching."

"On his land? Why didn't we go around?" Emily exclaimed.

"It's over a hundred thousand acres, ma'am. Would be a bloody long way around. Pardon my language."

The vastness of the properties was something Colin still couldn't quite wrap his head around. The riders arrived, and Colin, Patrick, Robbie, and Emily stood shoulder to shoulder, a united front, as the men dismounted. Colin's stomach had twisted into a knot.

"Good day." The man who was clearly the leader stepped forward, smiling. He was older, around sixty or so, and he lifted his leather hat to reveal cropped silver hair. Yet despite his age, he had a virility about him and gave off the impression of coiled power, waiting to strike. His friendly facade only made Colin's stomach churn even more.

Patrick spoke up. "Hello."

The man zeroed in on Patrick. "I'm Matthew Barnes, as you might have guessed. One of my boys spotted your little caravan out on his rounds." Barnes made an imitation of a laugh. "Lazy sods haven't finished the fence yet. Don't know what's takin' them so long, except maybe that I own half the territory."

The men chuckled dutifully, and Barnes extended his hand to Patrick. "Mr. Grant, I presume?"

Before Patrick could respond, Emily stepped forward and extended her own hand. "Mr. Grant is dead. I'm Mrs. Grant."

Barnes's eyebrows lifted for a moment before his face settled into a mask of sympathy. "I'm so terribly sorry for your loss, my dear." He took Emily's hand between both of his and patted gently. "It's a cruel world, isn't it?"

His men murmured their agreement. Colin suspected they'd agree with Barnes should he state the sky was green.

Emily removed her hand from his grasp. "Thank you, Mr. Barnes. I apologize for trespassing on your land, but it was an awful long way to go around." She smiled winningly.

Barnes returned her sunny expression, but Colin didn't believe him for a moment. "It's no bother at all, Mrs. Grant. As I said, I do own quite a large part of New South Wales. It would be my honor to show you around the place, my dear."

Emily was the very picture of a genteel lady. "That would be a delight, Mr. Barnes. Unfortunately, we truly do have to be moving on."

"Oh, of course. I know the challenges of herding cattle, that's for certain. I own ten thousand head myself. But my homestead is right on your way, I do believe. About twenty miles northward. Why don't you stop in for lunch tomorrow? I can send one of the boys to fetch you in my wife's carriage."

Colin certainly didn't like the idea of Emily going anywhere alone with Barnes, and he, Patrick, and Robbie all started to speak at the same time. Emily was quicker, however. "What a lovely offer! It would be my pleasure to join you and your wife for a meal. But there's no need to send the carriage. I'll make my own way."

"Whatever the lady desires. Say one o'clock?"

"I look forward to it very much." Emily smiled again, all feminine charm.

Barnes and his men doffed their hats to her and returned to

their horses, completely ignoring Colin, Patrick, and Robbie. As the men rode off, churning up a cloud of dust, Robbie shook his head. "Don't like him one bit, ma'am. You're not going alone."

Patrick spoke up. "Clearly a snake, that one."

Colin was in complete agreement. "Mrs. Grant, you shouldn't go. At least let us come with you."

Emily sighed, exasperated. "Gentlemen, I'm not going alone. Robert will come with me. You two will guard the herd. I don't trust him either."

"Oh. Well that sounds all right, I reckon." Robbie clapped his hands together. "Better get back to it."

Late the next morning, Robbie rode ahead to scout the location of Barnes's house. He returned and conferred with Emily, and they led the herd to a grassy spot near a shallow river. There were clumps of trees about, and the cattle grazed contentedly.

When Emily climbed from the back of the wagon, all three men stared, unable to mask their surprise. Colin had expected her to be outfitted in a fancy dress, but instead she wore men's clothing. Rather than her usual wide-brimmed sunbonnet, her hair was tucked up beneath an oiled leather hat. Her canvas trousers were cinched tightly with a knotted belt, and a too-big shirt was tucked in.

She seemed to be waiting for one of them to speak. "Do I look that ridiculous?"

Colin found his voice first. "No, no. Not at all, Mrs. Grant."

"They were Stephen's. I know they're too large, but I want to show that man that I'm not…"

"Easy prey?" Patrick suggested.

"Yes. Exactly." Emily looked to Robbie. "What do you think, Robert? Should I wear a dress?"

Robbie snapped out of his daze. "No, ma'am. I think you look…just right."

"Excellent. Colin, Patrick, you stay here and make sure the

herd is protected. I can't imagine Barnes would have any need for my cattle, but I suppose stranger things have happened. My rifle's under the seat in the wagon. I'm sure you won't need it, but just in case."

Patrick was disbelieving. "You're really going to leave us alone here? You're trusting us with a weapon?"

Emily nodded. "Yes. I think you've earned my confidence. Unless there's some reason I shouldn't have faith in you."

Colin spoke up. "Of course not. You can trust us."

"Very well. Shall we, Robert?"

Robbie tipped his hat. "After you, ma'am."

As Emily and Robbie rode off, Patrick leaned against a tree and ate a handful of nuts. He shook his head. "Silly woman. We could leave now and never look back."

Colin took a handful of nuts for himself, cracking the shells. "Where would we even go?"

"Back to the coast. Find some civilization."

Colin found the idea of leaving the drive decidedly unappealing. "I think we'd be the fools to give up an honest living with good people to go on the run as escaped convicts."

"Honest living? We're slaves, don't forget. Don't have two shillings to rub together."

"I know, but…I like it out here."

A smile teased Patrick's lips, and his eyes appraised Colin. "Mmm. It suits you, I must admit. They'd barely recognize you, the Lancasters."

Colin laughed. "Why, because I have reddened skin and I'm not in a frock coat?"

Patrick stood and approached Colin languidly. He reached out and removed Colin's hat, tossing it aside. "Not red anymore. Just darker. You don't look like a rich man's son." He inched closer and began unbuttoning Colin's shirt. "You're getting more muscles now." Patrick slipped Colin's shirt off and dropped it to the ground. He ran the tip of his finger down the center of Colin's chest.

His throat suddenly dry as a bone, Colin swallowed thickly. "I am?" He'd noticed his shirts were tighter, and he'd loosened his belt a notch.

Patrick's other hand came around and caressed Colin's back. "Aye. You are." Colin reached for him, but Patrick skipped away and glanced toward the river. "Let's take a dip. No one about but the cattle, and I don't think they'll mind."

Colin looked in all directions. The herd munched lazily, and they were alone as far as the eye could see. Excitement growing, he quickly followed, tossing the rest of his clothes by the riverbank and wading in after Patrick. They hadn't been able to couple again since the first time, and Colin was eager for more.

However, Patrick seemed in a teasing mood, and aside from a few stolen kisses, he slithered out of Colin's grasp as they splashed around. The sun was bright overhead, and they playfully wrestled with each other in the cool water. Colin tried to get a grip on Patrick, but Patrick evaded him time and time again, his laughter echoing over the water.

Finally Colin huffed in mock annoyance and retreated to a large, flat rock by the river's edge. He lay down on his stomach, folding his head on his arms. He closed his eyes and listened to the chirps of insects and the lowing of the cattle.

"Sulking now, are we?" Patrick teased.

Colin kept his eyes shut. "No. Just sunning."

A few moments later, he felt droplets of water on his back and Patrick's hand on his backside. "Careful, now. Your arse is still lily-white. Don't want to burn this delicate skin."

Before Colin could respond, he gasped at the sensation of Patrick slowly swiping his tongue across Colin's backside. Patrick's breath tickled his skin, and he traced patterns on Colin's cheeks with his fingers. Patrick settled himself behind Colin on the rock, lying flat against Colin's legs, which spread to accommodate him.

Anticipation glimmered in Colin's veins, and his cock grew beneath him. He was wondering what Patrick would do next when Colin felt his cheeks being parted, followed by Patrick's tongue flicking against his hole.

Shocked, Colin yelped, then groaned with sheer bliss as Patrick spread him open and lapped at him, tracing around the ridge of muscle and pushing inside Colin with this tongue. It was heavenly, and Colin soon panted for breath as Patrick pleasured him so very intimately. Colin hadn't known such an act existed, but as the sparks of delight brought his entire body to life, he was very glad it did.

His cock was now painfully hard below him, trapped against the hot surface of the rock. He shifted to try and take some of the pressure off, and a moment later, Patrick hauled him up onto the shore with strong hands. Colin rested on his hands and knees while Patrick disappeared. Colin opened his mouth to protest, but Patrick returned a moment later, close behind him.

Patrick prodded with slick fingers where his tongue had, and Colin moaned. "Please."

As he leaned over Colin, the head of Patrick's hard cock nudged Colin's entrance. "You want it?"

"Yes. God, yes. I want *you*."

With a low growl in his throat, Patrick thrust inside Colin, the burning friction making Colin seize up. Patrick's breath tickled Colin's ear, and his fingers skimmed down Colin's spine. "Relax for me. That's it. Let me in."

Taking a deep breath, Colin concentrated, allowing Patrick to move farther inside him. Patrick squeezed one of Colin's hips and pulled almost all the way out before pushing in again. "So tight," he muttered.

As the pain receded, Patrick seemed to sense it, and he began thrusting in a faster rhythm. Flickers of intense pleasure ricocheted in Colin's body, emanating from his ass and his cock. His arms quavered after a few minutes, and he went down on his elbows. This opened him up even farther to Patrick, who moaned loudly as he grasped Colin's hips with his hands, plunging into him ever deeper.

Colin realized the breathy gasps of pleasure he could hear were coming from him, and as Patrick leaned down and grasped Colin's leaking cock, Colin called out. Patrick stroked him roughly. "Yes. Let me hear you."

That they were out in the open in broad daylight added to Colin's exhilaration, and his cries of pleasure echoed. He let himself go, moaning noisily, which seemed to spur Patrick on. "God. Patrick. *Patrick*."

His hips slamming up against Colin's ass, Patrick stroked Colin's cock even faster, and a moment later, Colin's cries reverberated in the air as he came, spurting long, thick ropes on the ground and splashing up onto his chest. Colin flew apart, shaking as he clamped down on Patrick's cock. Patrick drove on, panting as he strove for his own release.

When Patrick found completion, he shuddered and filled Colin's ass with his hot seed. Colin collapsed on the grass, and Patrick followed, his weight heavy. Colin didn't mind, though. Patrick softened inside him but didn't withdraw. He pressed his lips against Colin's neck, and stroked Colin's hair idly.

After a few minutes, they made their way back into the river, washing themselves and moving into each other's arms for leisurely kisses. Colin was utterly content, and he wished the respite would never end. They took turns napping in the shade, limbs entwined. As Colin dozed, Patrick idly drew patterns on Colin's back. It was bliss.

Soon enough, however, Patrick spotted riders in the distance, and they dressed quickly. Squinting, Colin tried to make out if it was Emily and Robbie returning. He thought so but couldn't be sure. Patrick picked up the rifle, and they waited until the riders came into proper view. Colin heaved a sigh of relief when he saw Robbie's familiar form and Emily's small frame on the horse beside him.

They led their horses to the river to drink and dismounted. Emily removed her hat and wiped her forehead before taking a swig from her canteen. "Well, at least that's over."

"How did it go?" Colin asked.

"As well as can be expected. Mr. Barnes made it clear he doesn't think a woman has any place out here."

"Let the old bastard think what he wants, ma'am. You stood up to him mighty well."

"Thank you, Robert." Emily was fairly beaming. "He offered to buy my land. Well, 'offered' is probably too slight a word. More like he demanded I turn the deed over for whatever price he wanted. I politely declined."

Robbie grinned. "Thought his head was gonna explode. Face went all red. I could barely keep from laughin'."

"Yes, I expect Mr. Barnes is used to having his way. Not this time, I'm afraid." She addressed Colin and Patrick. "Everything all right here?"

"Yes, fine. Everything was fine." Colin was struck by guilt that he and Patrick hadn't exactly been watching the herd closely.

Emily seemed puzzled. "Are you sure?"

Patrick spoke up. "Quiet as a churchyard."

"Glad to hear it. We should keep moving. I'd like to get as far away from Mr. Barnes as possible." Emily brought her horse back to the wagon, and Robbie insisted on removing its saddle and hitching it back up for her.

They moved out, continuing across Barnes's land. A few hours later, Colin thought he saw a flare of light in the distance. He looked at Patrick to see if he'd noticed, and he didn't have to ask. Patrick's expression was grim. "Spyglass, I wager. Sun's reflecting off it."

A decidedly unpleasant thought crossed Colin's mind. "Do you think they were watching? Earlier?"

Patrick's jaw set, and he stared into the distance. After a moment, he shrugged and smiled slyly. "Hope they enjoyed themselves if they were. Gave them quite a show."

They shared a glance, and Colin flushed with renewed desire. He could hardly wait to do it again.

Chapter Eleven

WITH EACH PASSING day as they drew closer to their destination, Colin's anticipation grew. Robbie had regaled him with tales of Matthew Barnes's large home, and Colin hoped Stephen Grant had commissioned a house and outbuildings that would offer a degree of comfort.

It had been many months since he'd slept in a bed, and although he'd grown accustomed to the hard ground and long hours in the saddle, the thought of laying his head on a pillow once more was quite appealing.

One night after stopping the herd, Robbie took his rifle and rode off in search of food. Although Colin eagerly ate whatever Robbie managed to catch, he didn't think he could bear the thought of seeing the animal take its last breath. Instead he rooted about in some shrubs and small trees looking for fruit. One shrub bloomed with white flowers, and Colin bent to get a closer look.

"Shouldn't you be looking for food?"

Colin jumped at the sound of Patrick's voice. "Don't sneak up on people, Patrick Callahan."

"I thought you liked it when I get up close behind you." Patrick's words were heavy with innuendo.

Colin had to laugh. "Shhh. She'll hear."

"She's off in her own world." Patrick gazed down at the flowering shrub, which sprouted long stems with clusters of white flowers all along them. He reached down to touch one and yanked his hand back with a curse. "Damn it!" He waved his hand around in agitation.

"Thorns?"

Patrick didn't answer and swore under his breath, turning away.

"Stop. Let me see." Colin took hold of Patrick's arm and turned him around. With a sigh, Patrick held out his hand. An improbably large, hooked spike from the clever plant had deeply imbedded itself in the flesh at the base of Patrick's pointer finger. Colin leaned in and prodded gently.

"Just pull it out. It's nothing."

Colin quirked an eyebrow upward. "You're awfully agitated over nothing."

"I'm not agitated." Patrick tried to free his arm, but Colin held fast.

"Come. Sit." Colin knelt on the ground and tugged Patrick down beside him. He examined the troublesome spike and pinched it lightly. "Have to go slowly, or it'll break off and, with your luck, become infected."

"Bloody stupid flowers," Patrick grumbled. "Everything in this backward country is dangerous."

"Mmm hmm." Colin let him whine as he worked. "Did your grandfather make that ring himself?"

Patrick gazed at the darkened metal on his finger. "Aye. It's worthless, but…it's a piece of home."

Slowly but surely, Colin eased the spike out of Patrick's finger. Colin pressed against the small wound to stop the bleeding. "There you go."

It seemed Patrick couldn't resist a smile. "Aren't you going to kiss it better?"

"Many apologies. Of course." Colin lifted Patrick's palm and pressed his lips to it soothingly.

The brush crackled nearby, and they turned to find Emily standing a few yards away. Since the day she'd lunched with Matthew Barnes, she'd taken to wearing men's clothing every day. Her shirt was untucked and hung almost to her knees. She shook her head as she backed up. "I...I thought I'd help with the fruit." She turned and made her escape back to camp.

Colin still held Patrick's hand. They shared a resigned glance and parted. As they walked the short distance back to camp, several gunshots sounded in the distance. Robbie rarely missed, and it meant he would likely be returning shortly.

At camp, Emily was nowhere to be seen. Patrick pointed to the wagon, which had the back cover drawn. Robbie rode up a few minutes later, a wallaby slung over the back of his horse. He immediately sensed the tension. "What's happened?"

"Nothing." Colin shrugged, attempting to appear nonchalant.

Robbie peered between Colin and Patrick, who said nothing. Then he looked at the wagon. "Is she all right?"

Colin answered. "Yes. She's fine. Just resting, I suppose."

After a few moments, Robbie went about skinning the dead wallaby, a process that Colin could never bear to watch. Instead he worked on the fire, building it up. Robbie had taught him his fire-making techniques, and although Colin hadn't yet been able to start his own campfire, he had become adept at maintaining a fire once it was going.

As the meat cooked over the fire, Emily emerged. She said nothing to Colin or Patrick and took her spot by the fire. They ate in a silence punctuated by Robbie's occasional hunting stories. Colin, for one, was happy to let him chatter.

That night, Robbie was on watch, and Colin and Patrick set out their bedrolls near the fire, but more than a respectable distance from each other. On some nights when both in camp, they'd come together furtively, aware that Emily slept nearby in the wagon. But on this night, neither approached the other, and

Colin let the toll of the day's exertion overtake him into slumber.

When he woke the next morning, Robbie and Patrick weren't in the camp. Emily was perched nearby on a low rock, rolling up the long sleeves of her husband's shirt. Colin sat and took a swig of water from his canteen. He cleared his throat. "Good morning, Mrs. Grant."

"Good morning, Colin." She continued rolling up her left sleeve.

After a deep breath, Colin decided he should apologize. "I'm sorry for yesterday."

Emily finished with her shirt and gazed at him. "What do you have to be sorry for?"

Colin paused, unsure of the response she wanted. "Patrick and I…"

"You care for each other."

"Yes. I care for him very much." It was strange to say the words aloud. Colin wondered for a moment if he was still dreaming.

"I never considered it, you know."

Colin wasn't sure what she meant. "I'm sorry?"

"Of course I knew you were both sodomites. That's why you're here, after all. But you weren't what I expected. Certainly not you, especially. So well-bred. I imagine we might have met at a garden party if we'd been neighbors in England."

"Yes. I can imagine it easily."

"Instead here we are. Quite unlikely, but I suppose that's the way life unfolds sometimes, isn't it?"

Colin's life had certainly not gone to plan. "Yes."

"I'd always had the impression that men of your sort were base and immoral. Debauched. Animalistic."

Colin had no response. He waited for her to go on.

Surprisingly, Emily laughed quietly. "I'd actually forgotten for the most part. That you and Patrick are"—she was silent a moment—"different. Most days I'm so lost in my own world it's a feat that I notice anyone. But when I saw you yesterday…"

His stomach churned. "You remembered what godless creatures we are?"

Emily blinked in surprise. "No. I realized that you're quite the opposite. I'd never considered that two men could share genuine affection. And I'm sorry for that. I'm sorry for a great many things."

"I… You needn't be, Mrs. Grant." Colin had no idea what else to say.

"Call me Emily."

Colin smiled, pleased. "All right. Emily."

Hooves sounded, and Robbie and Patrick returned from whatever errand they'd been on. Emily watched them approach. "He is quite handsome, isn't he?"

"Yes. That he is." Colin smiled and got to his feet. "They both are," he added.

Emily looked startled. "Yes, I suppose." She stood and hurried to the wagon to ready the horses.

Patrick dismounted and gave Colin a questioning look. Colin spoke quietly. "Not to worry."

"Is she going to report us? Not that she saw anything that would hold up in evidence, but I doubt you need much out here." His expression was grim.

"No, no. She won't. She…understands."

Patrick snorted. "Understands? I doubt it. We'll see once they check up on us. Not that I can imagine the government coming all this way too often."

"I suppose they must."

"Hmm. Sometimes I wonder."

"It's all right, Patrick. We can trust Emily."

"'Emily,' is it now?" Patrick shook his head. "The only person I can trust is myself."

"What about *me*?" Colin straightened his spine as anger flared.

Robbie neared, and Colin turned and stalked over to Mission, irritated. Patrick had revealed so much more of himself over the months, but at the first sign of trouble, he seemed to shut down and erect his walls higher than ever.

They headed out, Colin's anger simmering as the morning wore on. The sun was a constant torment overhead, and he shifted restlessly in the saddle. Finally, when he felt he might scream with frustration, he rode over to Patrick. Robbie was up ahead, directing Emily, well out of earshot.

"I said, what about me?"

Patrick spared him a glance. "For God's sake. Let it rest."

"No. I won't. You don't trust me? After everything we've been through?"

Patrick's jaw set. "Don't make more of it than it is." He spurred his horse and cantered ahead.

Determined, Colin followed and reached over to yank Patrick's horse to a halt. "What is this between us?"

Patrick wrenched his reins back from Colin, and his horse shuffled in place. "A pleasant distraction."

Colin felt as if his heart was being squeezed painfully in his chest. "That's what I am to you. A distraction."

"We're trapped out here together. Might as well make the best of it."

"So you're just…*fucking* me to pass the time? Because I'm the only one out here who'll have you?"

Patrick exhaled sharply. "What do you want me to say? We enjoy each other. Slake our needs together. There's nothing wrong with that. But it's nothing more."

"I could be anyone to you, couldn't I? If Robbie was of a mind, you'd have him too." Colin shook his head, angry at himself for his delusions that Patrick had grown to care for him.

"You're damn right I would. You would too, if you had half a brain. You've got to forget these notions of…*romance*." He fairly spit the word out.

"Consider them forgotten. At least where you're concerned." Colin dug his heels into Mission's flanks and sped off to catch the herd, leaving Patrick in the dust.

THE DAYS TICKED by, a stony silence taking hold between Colin and Patrick. They spoke only when necessary and avoided each other when they could. When Colin and Robbie were alone one night after Patrick took watch, Robbie asked what had happened. Colin tried his best to shrug it off, and his expression must have been miserable enough that Robbie didn't press.

Part of Colin wanted to vent his frustration to Robbie, who was quite a good listener along with being an enthusiastic talker. Yet he was too embarrassed. He'd thought there was a deeper connection between Patrick and him, but it had simply existed in his imagination. Another fantasy that had carried him away, just like the books he'd once devoured.

As if in direct contrast to the chill between Colin and Patrick, the summer was upon them in all its brutality. The sweat stains on their clothing had become tinged with white, a sign of the salt being wrung from their bodies, according to Robbie. Colin became accustomed to waving one hand in front of his face whenever he was still to combat the flies that dived for his eyes, nose, and mouth, seeking moisture. The only relief came at nightfall, when the flies vanished as if into thin air and the heat abated.

The land was drier, and they had to ration their water supply. They ate the limes straight off the trees to quench their thirst and had to rest the cattle at the height of the day. As Robbie put it, there was no sense in getting to the station faster with half-dead cattle in tow.

Whereas Colin had once eagerly anticipated the nights for the chance to be alone with Patrick, now he craved the sunset solely for a respite from the sun and to sleep as much as possible. The nights on watch were the worst, since he had endless hours to muse over Patrick's lack of feeling for him. He wondered if Patrick missed him at all, but doubted he missed him more than Patrick would any other warm, willing body.

One stifling afternoon, Robbie whistled for Colin and Patrick from up ahead. Emily halted the wagon and gave Robbie a sour look as he hopped off his horse. "What is it, Robert?" Impatience and exhaustion warred in her curt tone. She swiped the sleeve of her husband's shirt across her face.

Robbie didn't answer, his gaze fixed on something on the ground before he looked off into the distance, first left, then right. You could see for miles in all directions, the land undulating with gentle swells punctuated by stark trees and rocky outcroppings.

He pointed to a shrub, and Colin wondered what he was going on about when he noticed the tattered piece of red material hanging limply from a wooden stake. "It's your land, ma'am."

A smile dawning on her drawn face, Emily jumped to her feet. There she wavered for a moment before tumbling off the wagon and onto the dusty earth. Robbie was at her side before Colin and Patrick could even dismount.

On his knees, Robbie tossed Emily's hat aside and leaned over her anxiously. He patted her cheek. "Ma'am, wake up. Open your eyes."

Colin watched helplessly. Finally Emily's eyelids fluttered, and she groaned and moved her head. Robbie sat back on his heels, exhaling in clear relief. "You stood up too quickly. It's the heat, ma'am."

Emily blinked and focused on Robbie. "Stop calling me that."

Robbie raised his eyebrows for a moment before smiling. "Only if you stop calling me by my proper name. No one's called me that…well, ever, really."

"All right. Robbie."

Patrick passed Robbie a canteen, and Robbie gently arched his arm around Emily's back to help her sit up and sip slowly. She wiped her mouth. "My apologies, gentlemen. I just felt rather faint all of a sudden."

Colin lifted his hat and wiped the sweat from his forehead. "I think we're all likely to swoon at sometime or other in this ridiculous heat."

Emily slowly found her footing, Robbie hovering close. She swatted the dirt from her trousers futilely. "We'll all need new clothing soon. Don't suppose there's a store nearby?"

"Not too far, ma—" Robbie remembered himself. "Emily."

"Only two hundred miles or so?" she asked teasingly.

"About three, actually. Due east. Town called Drayton. We can go stock up once the herd's settled on your station."

"How far to the homestead?" Patrick asked. "If this is her land we're standing on, we must be close."

"Not sure exactly. Only another day or two on the move, I reckon."

At this very welcome news, they all shared a smile. Colin met Patrick's gaze and for a lovely instant forgot his anger. But the moment soon passed, and Colin turned away, putting his attention back on the job at hand.

The very next morning, it was Colin's turn to end up flat on his back on the unforgiving ground.

Mission pranced around some cattle as Colin cracked his whip in the air, trying to drive the stubborn beasts out from under a large tree, the shade from its snarled branches offering the only haven from the sun.

Without warning, Mission reared up, whinnying loudly in distress. Clearly spooked by something, the horse bolted, and

Colin slid half out of the saddle, unbalanced and taken utterly off guard. Panic shot through him, and he yanked on Mission's reins, shouting a command to stop. The horse skidded and reared up again onto its back legs.

Although he clung to the animal with all his might, Colin was no match for gravity and momentum. He crashed to the ground, the air whooshing from his lungs. For a few moments, he felt paralyzed and stared at the clear, bright sky overhead as he willed his lungs to function.

The ground shook with a deafening thunder, and Colin feared he would be trampled by whatever approached. He ordered his limbs to move, yet they refused to comply. Fortunately, the noise stopped, and no hooves struck him. Patrick's face appeared overhead.

"Colin!" Patrick's expression was troubled.

Colin's response was a strangled attempt at speech.

With gentle hands, Patrick prodded Colin's arms and legs. "Is anything broken? Are you hurt?"

With what felt like a gargantuan effort, Colin was finally able to take a deep breath. Pain slashed across his back, but at least the paralysis was fading, replaced by soreness and embarrassment that he'd been unable to control his own horse. Although it made his skull ache, Colin moved his head in a tiny nod. "It's fine."

Patrick still poked and tested parts of Colin's body, one after the other. "Sure?"

The ground shook again, and soon Robbie leaned over Colin from the other side. "All right, mate?"

The shock worn off somewhat, Colin sat up gingerly. "Yes. Thank you."

Patrick stood and suddenly seemed unaccountably angry. "Be more careful." He stomped off to retrieve his horse, which had wandered to graze.

"Thanks for the concern," Colin muttered.

Robbie smirked. "You bet he was concerned." At Colin's doubtful expression, he added, "Couldn't get over here fast enough, could he? Like I said before. Mad about you. Just being bloody-minded is all." He winked and helped Colin to his feet.

Although he knew he should tamp it down, Colin couldn't help but feel a glimmer of hope.

ANY ILLUSIONS COLIN had harbored for a hint of the comforts of home once they reached the station were dashed as the homestead and outbuildings came into sight late that afternoon. A small, one-story wooden cabin sat atop a slight hill. Off to the side were several other buildings that could generously be called shacks. A rudimentary water tower stood sentry.

Emily rode ahead in the wagon, so Colin couldn't gauge her reaction, but he imagined she was as disappointed as he. As they approached, an aboriginal man and woman emerged from one of the smaller structures. The man was garbed in plain clothing, not unlike what Colin wore. The woman's dress was a simple red garment, and they were both barefoot.

By the time Colin, Patrick, and Robbie had settled the herd on a grassy area near a band of trees, Emily had already been speaking to the couple. She introduced them politely, although Colin could see the strain in her expression. This had not been what she expected. "Cobar and Tallara have been waiting for us."

Robbie extended his hand to Cobar first. Cobar peered at it with a blank expression before meeting it tentatively with his own hand. Patrick and Colin extended their hands in turn. Cobar was a small man, probably forty years old. Tallara was the same age, short and plump and with a wide face. She smiled, her eyes crinkling.

Patrick spoke up. "Is this all there is?"

Emily answered, her tone resigned. "Apparently so. My husband made all the arrangements through a man in Sydney. Stephen assured me I'd have all the comforts of home." She shrugged. "It would seem not."

Tallara spoke to Cobar in their own language. Cobar was apparently the only one of the two who spoke English. "Hungry?" he asked.

Colin's stomach growled at the thought, and Emily answered gratefully. "That would be wonderful. Thank you. It's been a long journey." She turned to address Colin, Patrick, and Robbie. "The main cabin is mine, obviously. Cobar and Tallara live in that building there. The last one is for you men. The smallest is storage, I'm told."

After collecting his meager belongings from the wagon, Colin headed over to their new quarters. The wooden door creaked inward to reveal a small cabin with bunks built into the walls on the left and right. For a moment, Colin had an unpleasant memory of the *Lady Harewood* and being kept like animals with the other men.

The cabin slept eight, four bunks on each side with a top and bottom. He dropped his sack on one of the lower beds, pleased at least to see there was a thin mattress and pillow. That alone would be a bit of luxury.

Now that they'd finally arrived, it was all rather disappointing, he found. Robbie and Patrick arrived and chose their beds, Patrick taking the lower bunk diagonal to Colin's on the other side of the undersized room. Robbie flung his pack on the upper bunk beside Colin. "Lavatory's out the back. Careful not to go in your bare feet. There might be scorpions out here."

Patrick seemed weary. "Along with the snakes and spiders."

"Yep." Robbie's usual good nature wasn't diminished in the slightest by the fact that the station was little more than a collection of hastily constructed wooden shacks.

"I suppose we shouldn't complain. Given that we're prisoners." Colin laid back and tested the mattress. It would be nice not to sleep on the ground, but he couldn't help but think of his room back home in England. It seemed a lifetime ago. Thoughts of Will and Rebecca crept in, unbidden. He wondered if he'd ever be able to mail the letters he'd written them.

They gathered in the main cabin for dinner, served up by Tallara. There was no table or chairs, so they sat on the dusty floor in a circle. Tallara placed the food in the middle on large leaves. Along with fruit, nuts, and meat that Colin thought was kangaroo, there were thick, tubular vegetables a few inches long. It seemed they were to eat with their hands, which Colin had become somewhat accustomed to, although they'd had wooden spoons on the trail for their stew.

He picked up one of the vegetables, which was a white color and seemed to be covered in a kind of ash from the cooking. He bit through the crispy outside, surprised to find the inside quite mushy. It was a light yellow and tasted a tad like almonds.

"How do you like it?" Robbie had an amused gleam in his eye.

Colin took another bite. "Tasty." He suddenly had a sinking feeling as he realized Robbie knew something he didn't. He swallowed thickly. "What is it?"

"Witchetty grub." Robbie pinched one between his fingers and took a hearty bite.

After taking a large gulp of water, Colin forced a smile on his face and picked up another grub. "Delicious!"

Tallara urged Colin to eat more. Patrick and Emily chuckled, and Cobar continued eating, paying them little attention for the most part. Emily gulped down a grub, as did Patrick. Robbie raised his canteen. "Now you're all real Australians!"

Laughing, Colin took another grub. Despite everything, he liked the sound of that.

Chapter Twelve

DECISIVELY CLOSING HIS eyes, Colin willed himself to sleep. He wore just his thin undergarments, finding the air in the cabin stifling. His back ached from his earlier tumble, and no position seemed comfortable.

It was the first night in his new home, and Colin wished he could feel settled. Yet the minutes crept by, and his brain wouldn't stop whirling. He listened to Robbie snore and wondered if Patrick was asleep yet. Colin knew he should just ignore Patrick altogether but found it impossible.

The answer of whether Patrick slept yet was soon answered by a rustle of clothing and his stealthy approach to where Colin lay. Colin kept his eyes shut, even as Patrick perched beside him. There was a soft laugh and whisper. "I know you're awake."

Sighing, Colin opened his eyes. Patrick was shirtless, and the moonlight caressed the planes of his chest. "What do you want?"

"Feeling all right? That was quite a fall."

"Yes. Fine." In truth, Colin was sure he'd be painted with bruises tomorrow.

"Liar." Patrick leaned close. "I'll help you feel better." He reached down and squeezed Colin's cock gently through the thin cotton covering him.

Colin grasped Patrick's wrist. "No."

"What, him?" Patrick glanced up at Robbie. "He's dead to the world."

"No. Not him. *You.*"

Patrick compressed his lips and whispered, "How long are you going to keep this up? I'm sorry, all right?"

"No. I might as well be a farm animal to you. This is all you want me for."

"For pity's sake. Forget these flowery notions and be a man."

Enraged, Colin bolted upright and took Patrick's arm, shaking it roughly as he hissed, "I *am* a man. My own man. For the first time in my life, I'm a part of something. I have skills. I'm needed. I'm a proper stockman. A *good* one. I'm not an aimless child any longer!"

"Prove it, then." Patrick reached down and boldly squeezed Colin's cock.

"No!" Colin shoved Patrick's chest with both hands and whispered, "*No.*"

Patrick huffed in irritation. "Fine. Be a stubborn mule." He stalked back to his bed and rolled toward the wall, his back to Colin.

Sleep was now certainly the furthest thing from Colin's mind as he stewed over Patrick's nerve. How dare *he* get upset? Colin stared at the uneven roof and fumed. It was going to be a very long night.

ON THE JOURNEY from Sydney, Colin had focused on reaching the station and hadn't much considered what they'd find there. The answer, it turned out, was endless work. Aside from caring for the herd and making sure they were fed and watered and healthy, fences needed to be built, and that required materials. With Cobar in the lead, they filled their days with felling suitable trees, sawing the wood into the sizes they needed, and transporting it.

According to Robbie's estimation and the map Cobar had drawn, Emily's station, which still had no name, was roughly seventy miles square. For now they had built a large horse paddock and temporarily penned in the herd over a field that stretched out beyond the main cabin. The herd would need to move regularly to find fresh grass to eat. A riverbed ran through a long portion of the property, although it was dry in summer.

Aside from caring for the herd and growing it, they had to build a permanent fence around the perimeter of the station property. It would take months, if not years.

Colin and Patrick coexisted peacefully enough, each man seeming to take care not to pay much attention to the other. Colin threw himself into the work, which he enjoyed despite the harsh conditions. He found a satisfaction in working with his hands that he had never experienced in all his years of study.

After a long day of felling trees with Robbie, Colin changed his sweat-soaked shirt and gratefully drank a fruit juice Tallara gave him. The sky turned vibrant orange, tinged with pink, as the sun set. The flies disappeared, and the air was remarkably cooler within mere minutes. Australia was nothing if not a land of extremes.

Cobar and Patrick headed out on foot in the fading light. Patrick seemed to have taken an interest in hunting, or perhaps his interest lay simply in being as far away from Colin as possible. Although he knew Cobar was married to Tallara, Colin couldn't help but feel a stab of jealousy. He wondered why Robbie didn't accompany them as he watched them disappear into the bush.

Tallara was cooking supper, and the delicious aromas made Colin's stomach rumble. He wandered over the gentle rise beyond the cabin and spotted Robbie and Emily by the herd's pasture. Robbie seemed agitated about something and abruptly stalked off as Colin approached.

Emily perched on the new fence surrounding the cattle, and

Colin pulled himself up beside her. He patted the wood. "We didn't do a bad job."

Emily was clearly troubled, her thoughts elsewhere. "Hmm? Yes, I'm pleasantly surprised, I must admit."

"Is everything all right? I didn't mean to interrupt."

Her laugh was forced. "Interrupt? No, of course not."

Although quite unconvinced, Colin changed the subject. "You know, I think we'd be lost without Cobar and his way around the bush. Seems like he can find whatever we need before we even know we need it. I can't imagine how we'll find enough wood the right size to go around the whole station, though."

"One piece at a time."

"Yes, I imagine so."

She gazed at the horizon, where the moon slowly emerged. "Sometimes I can hardly believe it's the same sun and moon in the sky. Everything here is so much bigger, somehow."

"Truly. England seems so miniscule. So distant now. Like another life. Which it was, I suppose." He gazed up at the darkening sky. "Even the constellations are different here. Sometimes it's as if we're on another planet altogether."

Staring into the distance, Emily spoke almost as if Colin wasn't present. "I never wanted to come here. It was Stephen's grand ambition. To be a pioneer. I suggested America, but he declared it was too full of people already. He wanted to blaze new trails. He got the idea in his head of becoming a rancher. So here I am." Her smile was heartbreaking. "And he lies at the bottom of the sea."

"But look at what you've accomplished. You're the bravest woman I know. I can't imagine what you've been through."

Emily's eyes glistened. "As he died, I promised him I'd see it through. The station, the cattle, all of it. But I'm not brave, Colin. I'm weak. So very, very weak. Faithless."

Colin wanted to reach out but wasn't sure if he should.

"You're far too hard on yourself, Emily."

"No. I'm an awful woman. You have no idea."

"What is it you think you've done?" Colin was perplexed as to where this was coming from. "You've honored your husband's wishes as he never could have hoped."

"I loved Stephen so much. I did. Truly." She sniffed and wiped her eyes uselessly as more tears spilled over.

"Of course you did." Colin was still mystified but didn't press.

"It's just…as you said, it feels like another life. It's been naught but months, but he's receded so far into the distance." She looked away, and her voice was barely more than a whisper. "I've felt so adrift and he was there, and…it was a comfort."

After a moment, Colin realized the "he" in question was not her husband. He'd been so preoccupied with his own romantic entanglement that he hadn't been paying attention to anyone else. "Robbie?"

Emily nodded miserably. "Just the one night. Yet I can't stop thinking of him. He makes me feel alive again."

Colin was actually quite pleased by the news. "I don't see the wrong in it. You're still alive. You're young. Surely your husband would have wanted you to be happy?"

She stared at him, shocked. "Don't see the wrong? It's wicked! I'm thirty-eight years. Old enough to be his mother! Can you imagine what people would say?" She buried her head in her hands.

Colin glanced at the vast emptiness around them. "Who, Emily? We're not in England."

She wiped her eyes. "I know, but…surely you of all people understand? When I think of what my family would say…"

"Of course I understand. My parents would die of shame to see me performing menial tasks. Factor in my *wicked* nature and they'd both have the vapors."

Emily looked down at herself. "I think the trousers alone

would give my mother need of smelling salts." She shook her head. "I can't help but worry about their opinions."

"I know. But our families aren't here. Nor are the gossiping ladies at Sunday church. Who here will judge? Patrick and me? Cobar and Tallara?" I think I can safely say none of us will think badly of it. Robbie's been smitten since the day you met."

She glanced up. "Really?"

Colin smiled softly. "I was usually too busy with Patrick to think on it, but looking back, Robbie's fancied you for quite a while."

Happiness flickered across her face for a moment, but she shook her head doggedly. "It's madness. He's a fine young man, but he needs a woman he can have a future with."

"He can't have a future with you?"

"An old widow? What kind of life would that be? Surely he wants children."

Colin didn't want to pry and ask why Emily didn't have any children of her own, though he'd idly wondered about it before. "Have you spoken to him about it?"

"No. He's keen to talk, but I've avoided him at every turn."

"Ah. Patrick seems to be taking a page from your book." Colin knew he'd pushed him away and wasn't being entirely fair, but he silenced that inner voice.

Emily placed her hand on Colin's arm. "What happened between you? I didn't want to pry."

Shrugging, Colin tried to laugh but didn't quite make it. "Nothing. Apparently everything we shared was…nothing. To him, anyway."

"I'm sorry to hear that." She grew quiet for a long moment, clearly troubled. "Colin, there's something else I must confess."

"All right. Although I still don't see anything wrong with you and Robbie together."

"I think you'll feel differently about this." After taking a deep breath, Emily exhaled slowly. "Please understand that I never meant any harm. I was frightened and overwhelmed, and I let myself be manipulated."

Colin wasn't sure what was coming, but he grew increasingly apprehensive. "What's this about?"

"The government isn't going to check on you. As far as they're concerned, you're not even in Australia."

This was certainly not what Colin expected. "I'm sorry? I don't understand."

"When we were on that ship and Stephen died, at first I thought I'd turn around and take the first voyage back. I couldn't fathom going on." She paused, seeming to struggle with her thoughts. "I was alone. One of the crew told me how difficult it is in the colony to find labor. It was all so overwhelming."

Colin was wary. "Go on."

"Once I decided that I wouldn't turn around and run back home, I knew I needed help. Some prisoners, if they have the skills, can be placed with settlers, but they said there was a mile-long list and I'd wait months at the minimum. This man knew one of the guards, and he said they could arrange something with an official in Sydney. So I paid them. For you and Patrick."

"You…bought us?" Colin was stunned.

"It sounds so dreadful when you put it like that. I was desperate. I'd gotten it in my head that I needed to do this. For Stephen. I didn't think anyone would get hurt. You were strangers to me. Convicts. Sinners. I never thought of you as…"

"Human?" Colin asked. There was a hollowness in his chest.

"But you weren't at all what I expected. That day in the store, you asked for paper and ink to write home and you were both good men, kind men, and I wanted to tell you the truth, I did. But I was ashamed and afraid, and I didn't know what to do." Her words spilled out on top of each other in a rush.

Shocked, Colin wasn't sure how to feel. He honestly forgot

sometimes that he and Patrick were still prisoners. Still, he'd thought of Emily as a friend, and the fact that she'd deceived him slashed deeply. "When were you going to tell us?"

Emily seemed to be struggling for the right words. "I…I don't know. I hadn't planned it, and I told myself I would. When the time was right. I'm so sorry, Colin."

"Where does this leave us? Patrick and I?"

"The ship's record was doctored, and your papers destroyed. You're free to go. And I'll pay you for all your work. Whenever you want to leave, I'll help you as much as I can."

Leave. Colin had no idea where he'd go. The possibilities flickered by in his mind—back to Sydney, another part of Australia, return to England. None were appealing whatsoever, he found. It had taken so long to get to the station, and he was certain he didn't want to leave it now. "And if I want to stay?"

Emily's smile was shocked and hopeful. "You'd stay? Truly?"

"Yes. I want to build this station. Make it great. Make it something to be proud of." Colin had never felt such a sense of purpose in his life. "I don't care about the money. I have everything I need here."

"I will pay you, of course, for all your work. We'll sort it all out once the herd grows and we can make some profit."

"Agreed."

Emily's eyes swam with tears once more. "You're one of the finest men I've ever known. I promise I'll earn your trust. I'll make it right. I'll tell Patrick tonight and—"

"No! Don't tell him." Colin gathered himself after his outburst. "What I mean is…not yet. Don't tell him *yet.*"

She was silent for a few moments. "Because he won't want to stay."

Colin shook his head. "No. He won't. His pride wouldn't allow it. He'd go and never return." He knew he was being unspeakably selfish, but no matter how angry he might be with

Patrick, the idea of never seeing him again was untenable. "Just for now. We'll tell him when the time is right."

"Once things are more...settled between you."

"Yes. Then we'll tell him everything." That voice inside told him that he should be honest now and not keep Patrick in the dark, but he smothered it.

"He does care for you very much, you know. He can be a hard man, but he doesn't hide his feelings as well as he'd like." She pulled out a handkerchief from her pocket and blew her nose. "Matters of the heart are always so dreadfully complicated. We're quite a pair, aren't we?"

Colin gently wrapped his arm over her shoulders, and she melted against him. The stars were brightening in the clear sky overhead. "Yes, I suppose we are."

"Thank you for understanding. I couldn't imagine it here without you now."

He squeezed her affectionately. He didn't see the sense in being angry with her deception. He likely would have ended up in far worse circumstances if not for Emily. "You still need to think of a name, you know. For the station."

"Nothing's come to me yet. Any suggestions?"

"I think you'll know it when you hear it."

Leaning against each other as the stars brightened, they watched the sky, full with possibility.

AFTER A MORNING of tending to the herd and ensuring the animals were healthy and content, Colin and Patrick moved on to fencing. They worked in silence broken only by the odd grunt of exertion.

The sun was unfettered by even the slightest hint of a cloud. Colin felt as if he might never feel rain on his skin again. He marveled that anything grew on the bone-dry land at all. Cobar had told him the rain would come in winter, but Colin could barely imagine it.

"Never thought I'd miss the rain." Patrick gulped from his canteen. It was as if he'd read Colin's mind.

"Or the damp that seeps right into your bones."

"Never sounded quite so good."

Patrick walked over to a low stack of wood Robbie or Cobar had left earlier. His boot kicked one of the small logs, and it tumbled to the ground. A flash of movement caught Colin's eye, and he cried out as Patrick bent to retrieve the log. "No!"

Patrick froze. The snake that had been curled in the woodpile slithered away in a flash, retreating into the dry shrubbery. It had looked a most ordinary brown color, which Robbie had warned was one of the most deadly snakes of all.

Colin had instinctively rushed to Patrick's side, and gripped Patrick's waist, the other hand on his shoulder. Patrick whistled as he straightened. "There's another thing I miss. No bloody snakes in Ireland."

As the burst of panic faded, Colin managed a smile. "We need your namesake to pay a visit and drive the miserable creatures from this island too."

Patrick peered over his shoulder as his hand covered Colin's on his waist. "Looks as if you rescued me again."

They were only inches apart, and Colin leaned into Patrick, his body moving seemingly of its own accord. The brims of their hats bumped, and Patrick tossed his to the ground as he turned, snaking his arms around Colin's back. Colin knew he should move away, but the heat from Patrick's body and the bald desire in his gaze melted Colin's defenses.

"Want you." Patrick ran his thumb over Colin's lower lip, sending blood rushing to his cock.

The sound of an approaching horse broke the spell, and Colin stumbled back. As Robbie rode up, Patrick swore under his breath and jammed his hat back on.

"How's it going?" Robbie asked far too cheerfully.

Colin mumbled a reply, and soon they went back to the task at hand, silent once more.

UNABLE TO SLEEP that night, Colin dressed silently in the dark. Robbie had turned in early after saying barely two words all evening. Colin wasn't sure whether to commiserate with him or give Robbie his space, and in the end said nothing. There was silence from Patrick's side of the cabin, where Colin could make him out, curled on his side toward the wall.

Closing the door gently behind him, Colin breathed deeply of the cool night air and walked toward the pasture. All was quiet but for the scuttle of the odd animal in the nearby bush. Colin passed the herd and kept walking until he came to an old tree atop a wooded slope. He sat and leaned against it, drinking in the night.

A spot of exercise and fresh air was evidently the cure for his insomnia, and his eyes soon grew heavy. The crackle of movement in the dry undergrowth snapped Colin wide awake a few moments later. Eyes wide, he gazed about in the darkness, standing slowly. Breath shallow, he told himself it was merely a stray wallaby or piglike wombat. Or perhaps some other creature he hadn't come across yet. Preferably harmless.

There was a footfall, and a figure emerged from amid the trees. Patrick.

Colin knew him at a glance, even in the shadows. He exhaled, the tension in his limbs releasing. "Announce yourself next time."

Patrick halted a few feet away. "Apologies, Lord. Did you think I was something coming to eat you?" His tone was light and teasing.

Colin reminded himself that he was angry and that Patrick's charm didn't change that. "What do you want?"

Stepping closer, Patrick reached for him. "Come now. Let's not quarrel."

Colin stepped from his grasp. "Go away. There's nothing else to say."

"There is, actually."

"What, another lecture? I know your philosophy, Patrick. Trust only yourself. I still don't agree and I never will."

"I was wrong."

This was certainly not the response he had anticipated, and it stopped him short. "Pardon?"

"I said, I was wrong."

"Words I never thought I'd hear from your lips." Colin remained guarded. "What's brought this on?"

"Narrowly escaping a murderous snake would make any man take stock. I've had enough. Avoiding each other. Being angry. To what end?" He inched closer, gaze intense. "I do trust you, Colin. It doesn't come easily to me. But I do." He reached up, fingertips like a feathery kiss on Colin's cheek. "When the fever took me, there were times I could hear your voice. Feel your touch. I remember knowing I was…safe."

Colin leaned into Patrick despite himself. "Why are you telling me now?"

"Because I don't want to spend another night not having you in my bed."

Stepping back, Colin shook his head. "That's all you care about."

Patrick caught him about the waist. "*And* because it's the truth." He looked at Colin seriously. "When I was ill, I knew deep down that you'd protect me. Just as you did that night, going against your father and the men who wanted to wring my neck. So yes, Colin. I do trust you."

Guilt nipped at him. Here Patrick stood, telling Colin he had his trust, when Colin was keeping Emily's truth from him. *He'll leave you. He doesn't need to know, not now. What good will it do?* Colin wanted nothing more than to fall into Patrick's arms. "And you admit that this—this thing between us—it's more than physical. More than amusement. More than passing time."

"Aye. 'Tis."

Seemingly of their own accord, Colin's arms stole around Patrick's waist, his heart soaring at Patrick's confession. The guilt gnawed harder, teeth sharp as he stared into Patrick's eyes. *Tell him.* Colin took a breath, but the words evaporated. He'd tell him soon. *Soon.*

Then they were kissing, mouths open, tongues questing as they fit their bodies together, coming alive. All other thoughts vanished, and Colin drank Patrick in as he had the night air earlier—the taste of his mouth, the stroke of his tongue, the low moans in his throat that vibrated and seemed to go straight to Colin's cock. It was headier than any wine he'd ever sipped.

Patrick drew back, and Colin gulped the cool air before leaning in to kiss him again. He felt as if he'd been dying of thirst in the cruel sun and now he'd found the sweetest water. Patrick held him close, hands stealing up below Colin's shirt, roaming over his skin.

Colin moaned in protest when Patrick tore his mouth away, but soon quivered with excitement as Patrick sank to his knees, his hands quick on Colin's belt and trousers. Colin was already hard, and his cock curved upward as Patrick stroked it teasingly. Looking up, Patrick's smile was mischievous as Colin bucked his hips eagerly. Patrick ran his tongue along the pulsing vein on the underside of Colin's cock, his fingers dancing over Colin's bollocks.

Groaning, Colin submitted to the delicious torment, leaning back against the thick trunk of the gum tree. He longed for release, but Patrick's touch was tenaciously nimble, teasing him and stoking the desire that pooled in his belly until Colin was sure he'd explode with wanting.

As Patrick slipped his tongue into the slit at the end of Colin's cock, Colin reached out and tangled his fingers in Patrick's hair, urging him on. Relenting, Patrick took him into the moist heat of his mouth, sucking forcefully. Where moments before it had been all lightness and skimming touches, now Patrick's mouth stretched as he took Colin in deeply.

As Patrick opened his throat, Colin pumped his hips forward, thrusting in. His own harsh moans and breaths were loud in the still of the night as he took control, possessing Patrick's mouth, grasping his head in place as he pushed into the tight, wet pressure, his cock throbbing.

Patrick swallowed around him as Colin drove in, grunting as the flickers of pure bliss fanned into flames that spread out from his cock. He thought about what it would be like to mount Patrick and ride him, to pulse inside him as he was now inside his soft, wet mouth. With a shudder and final thrust, Colin came, shooting down Patrick's throat. He emptied, head thrown back, eyes closed as his body quaked with ecstasy.

His fingers loosening in Patrick's hair, Colin slipped from his mouth. Boneless and panting, he sank to his knees, his trousers tangled around his feet. He could make out glistening strings of his seed on Patrick's swollen lips and kissed him deeply, tasting himself. He reached for Patrick's cock, but found it soft and wet.

Chuckling, Patrick shrugged. "My hand was free once you took over."

Colin laughed softly and ran his thumb along Patrick's lower lip. Although Patrick had pleasured Colin with his mouth before, he'd always remained firmly in control. If Patrick's words hadn't convinced Colin of his trust, his actions had.

A stab of shame at his deception returned, most unwelcome.

Colin shifted and stifled the troublesome guilt.

Patrick caressed Colin's cheek. "What is it?"

"Naught." Smiling, Colin kissed him tenderly and settled into Patrick's arms.

He'd tell him when the time was right.

Chapter Thirteen

DAYS PASSED, THE work as challenging as ever, yet Colin barely felt his body's aches and pains. He and Patrick stole away together at least once a day, sometimes slipping off into the bush while building fences or creeping out past a sleeping Robbie at night.

Colin had hoped to see Robbie spending more nights with Emily, but it seemed she was determined to keep him at arm's length. Robbie's usual good humor was scarce, and although he did his work without complaint, he spoke only when spoken to and kept to himself as much as possible.

While Colin was sorry for his friends' troubles, he felt as though he was walking on air through the long days. Just the simple brush of Patrick's hand on Colin's back could spark desire, leading to furtive kisses in the shade of a stand of trees, or bodies pressing together on the dusty red earth.

Patrick drew up plans for an eventual stable at the station, describing it in such detail one afternoon as they rested below a rocky ridge that Colin could practically smell the musty hay and feel an apple in his pocket. He was delighted by Patrick's excitement for the project. "I've always dreamed of having you in a stable. Well, of you having *me*."

His eyes darkening with need, Patrick kissed Colin's smile away, his mouth branding him, hard and deep. Soon their hats and shirts were at their feet in the shade of the ridge as they devoured each other. Patrick spun him around and hauled Colin back against his chest, grinding into him. Taking Colin's hands in his own, he spread them wide on the red rock face, bending him over and yanking his trousers down.

Breathing heavily, Colin arched his back as Patrick thrust into him, the burn of pleasure mixed with pain. "Yes. *Yes.*" Colin gasped, all his nerve endings seemingly centered in his ass as it was stretched with Patrick's throbbing cock. With no grease to smooth the way, the friction was raw and incredible.

Sweat dripped into Colin's eyes, and he was consumed by the scorching heat of Patrick inside him, pounding into him relentlessly. Patrick's fingers on Colin's hips would leave marks, and Colin's mind took him back to that day long ago in the stable, watching Patrick mount the groundskeeper. A low moan escaped his lips, and Patrick's teeth nipped his shoulder.

Colin pushed back, panting, eager for more, meeting Patrick's powerful thrusts. Patrick leaned over him, angling down and slamming in even deeper. His right hand covered Colin's on the rock, their fingers clutching as they ascended to even greater heights, straining together.

His cock rigid and pulsing, Colin shook as Patrick reached around and stroked it roughly. Patrick grunted, his harsh breathing hot on Colin's ear. "Come for me." Every muscle in Colin's body strained as he strove for completion. "Only for me."

Crying Patrick's name, Colin shuddered, his toes curling as the heat ripped through him, searing him from the inside out. He clamped down on Patrick's cock, and after one more thrust, Patrick plunged over the edge, jolting as he emptied inside Colin. Colin's knees buckled, but Patrick caught him about the waist with strong hands. He eased him down to the ground, hastily spreading out their discarded shirts.

Catching his breath, Colin stretched out on his side and pillowed his head on his arm. His trousers were still caught around his boots, but he couldn't muster up the energy just yet to pull them up. Colin was utterly content as Patrick pressed tender kisses to his well-used bottom. He felt open and raw, desirable and wanted.

"I suppose we should get back to our tasks," Colin mused, although what he really wanted to do was nap. His limbs felt far too heavy to move.

Patrick gently rolled Colin onto his back. "Mmm. Should really clean up first." He dipped his head and licked lazily across Colin's belly, which was sticky with his own seed. Colin shivered, his eyes closing. It didn't seem they'd be back at work for quite some time.

ONE TYPICALLY BRIGHT morning a few days later, Colin and Cobar worked together on the never-ending fence. A bright red bird cawed and flapped out of a tree with a burst of energy as they approached with their tools. The wood for the fence had been taken out by wagon that morning and awaited them in neat stacks.

Amazingly the summer heat seemed only to be intensifying. He couldn't recall the last time he'd seen rain, and the flies were a near constant irritation that grated on his nerves. He waved them from his face and gulped from his canteen. "Don't they drive you mad?"

Cobar was unperturbed as ever and shook his head.

"Years of experience dealing with them, I suppose. I hope to find them less bothersome any day now." Colin swatted one from the corner of his eye. It landed on his lip a moment later, and he brushed it off.

"No insects on your land?"

"In England? There are, but not like you have here. Everything is much smaller and less deadly." Colin took another drink and lifted his hat to scratch his head. Emily had cut his hair for him, and it was a relief to have it out of his eyes once more.

"Miss home?" Cobar asked.

Colin was caught off guard. He pondered the question for a long moment. "Sometimes." He wondered what his parents were doing and if they thought of him at all. He supposed they were doing the same things they'd always done. The notion that he'd never see them again cut surprisingly deep, and when he least expected it.

"I would miss home." Cobar drank from his own canteen.

"Yes, I'm sure you would. Tell me, what did your people think when the British first arrived?"

"I'm told they wondered if the pale men were the ghosts of our ancestors, returning from the other world."

Colin's chuckle was rueful. "What a disappointment we must be."

Cobar seemed to ponder this and took his time before answering. "Some wish you would return to your home. We share the land, but you want to own it. This is not our way."

Colin had honestly never considered it. "But why do you and Tallara work for Emily if you don't feel anyone should own property?"

"We cannot stop you, so we keep it safe. Keep our sacred places untouched."

"Oh." Again, Colin hadn't even stopped to consider it. Shame roiled his stomach. "I'm sorry. It must seem so odd to you. Building a fence."

"Yes."

"I hope you know we'd never purposefully do anything to disrespect your people or the land. I certainly wouldn't. Nor would the others, I'm sure."

Cobar regarded him for a long moment that soon stretched out uncomfortably. Swatting at another squadron of flies, Colin shifted from foot to foot, his cheeks growing hot under Cobar's gaze. Then Cobar turned back to his work. Colin tried to think of the right thing to say, but found there was nothing.

AFTER DINNER THAT night, Cobar and Tallara retired to their cabin. The work at the station was from sunrise to sunset, and they rarely had late nights. Colin, Robbie, Patrick, and Emily sat around the floor with the map Cobar had drawn of the station property, discussing the fencing strategy before bed.

Robbie shrugged. "It's going to take a fair amount of time to put the fence up. Fencing's a slow business."

"Do you think I should hire more men?" Emily asked.

Robbie shrugged again. "Up to you, ma'am."

"I'm asking for your opinion, Robert."

"Why? Doesn't matter what I think about anything else."

Colin hated seeing his friends at odds. "Of course it matters."

"Perhaps you'll get more free prison labor if you're lucky," Patrick suggested testily.

Colin shifted nervously. He knew it was time Patrick learned the truth, but everything had been going so well. He hated to upset the balance. *Just wait a bit longer.*

Robbie spoke. "Didn't you say they'd be visiting? The government people. We should make sure we're here when they do. Wouldn't want them thinking Colin and Patrick have run off. When do you expect them?"

Emily fidgeted and stared at the map. "I don't know, exactly. We shan't worry about it. Let's focus on the matter at hand."

As Patrick's gaze narrowed on Emily, a warning signal went off in Colin's mind. Patrick's tone was razor-sharp. "Shouldn't we have heard something by now? We're miles away from civilization, but I didn't think the colony was in the habit of losing track of convicts."

Emily didn't look up. "I'm sure they'll come around sometime or other. So, about the fence—"

"What aren't you telling us?" Patrick straightened his spine, and his jaw tightened.

Emily shook her head, eyes still on the map. "Nothing. Robbie, what do you think about—"

Patrick slammed his fist onto the dusty floor. "Look me in the eye and tell me you're not lying."

Robbie pushed up to his knees. "All right. That's enough."

Colin glanced between Patrick and Emily, his heartbeat accelerating, sweat breaking out on his palms. *Not yet. Not yet. More time.* Emily's gaze was still rooted to the floor. Colin stayed frozen, afraid to even move.

Emily closed her eyes, and when they fixed on Patrick, tears shone. "I didn't know what else to do. You have to understand."

"Understand *what*?" Patrick's temper was only barely contained.

"One of the guards and the crew arranged it for me. I needed men, and they told me I'd have trouble finding good workers in Sydney. So instead I got you and Colin."

Patrick's nostrils flared. "For a price."

Emily's expression was etched with regret. "They have some sort of…scheme going on. Only one or two prisoners per ship. The paperwork is destroyed, so there's no record. I paid them and in return…"

Patrick finished for her. "You got a couple of slaves."

"But you must know how much I've grown to care for you. Sincerely."

Robbie spoke up. "When were you going to say something?" He was clearly affected by Emily keeping the truth from him, disappointment creasing his face.

Patrick's laugh was discordant. "Never! That's when. She was just going to use us for as long as she liked." His accusing gaze settled on Robbie. "Sure you didn't know? *Mate*?"

Robbie looked Patrick straight in the eye. "No. I didn't." Then he gazed at Emily with a terribly sad expression.

"You bitch." Patrick's fury boiled over, and Colin's panic intensified as he watched the scene unfold.

Robbie's voice rose. "Don't." He seemed poised to tackle Patrick if need be, his hackles raised. "Emily made a mistake. But put yourself in her spot for a moment and—"

"I'd love to! She's got more money than I'll ever see. She's got her freedom." Patrick jumped up and paced furiously. "Let me get it straight. Our paperwork's gone? No one's coming to check up on us?"

Emily answered. "That's right. They said it would be like you don't exist."

"Well, then at least we can thank you for that, Mrs. Grant." Patrick nodded to Colin as he turned on his heel. "Come on."

Colin's mind raced as he jumped to his feet and followed. "Wait!" The night sky was luminescent overhead, and a gentle breeze wafted on the air. Colin wished he could take Patrick down to the pasture and kiss the anger from him, but he felt as though a sea change was taking place and he was helpless to slow its momentum.

"Patrick, stop." Colin grabbed his shoulder, but Patrick spun out of his grasp.

"I should have known the government would never let us wander so far from their clutches. I can't believe I didn't see it right away. Neither of us did."

"I..." Colin grappled to find the right words. Emily hadn't let on that he already knew the truth, and it would be so easy to keep that fiction going. Yet he knew he couldn't. He should have told

Patrick the truth as soon as he knew it. He opened his mouth to tell him everything but knew it was too late. Patrick could read it all over his face.

Patrick's wrath faltered, and for a sickening moment, he stared at Colin with such utter hurt and disbelief. "You knew."

"I was going to tell you; I swear!" Colin reached for him, imploring, but Patrick tore his arm from Colin's grasp.

"How long?"

"Patrick—"

"How long have you known?" Patrick shouted, fists clenched.

"Not long. Weeks. I was going to tell you."

"Aye? When, exactly?"

"When the time was right." Colin's answers sounded pathetic even to his own ears.

"In the meantime, you thought you'd just keep me on my leash."

"No! It wasn't like that."

"I'm a bloody fool." Patrick shook his head, muttering. "Let down my guard. Let myself become *complacent*." He spit the word out like it was poison.

"*Happy*, you mean?" Colin stepped closer. "We've been happy here. You can't argue with that."

"Doesn't matter. Can't stay now." Patrick's jaw clenched. "I should never have trusted you. Should have known better."

"Where would you go?" Colin wished he'd wake up from this nightmare. Patrick was slipping from his grasp, and he'd brought it on himself.

"Anywhere! To hell with this place. To hell with *her*. And you."

"Is it really so terrible?" Colin's thoughts and emotions churned in his mind, hopelessly muddled. "I'm not glad Emily lied to us. But I wouldn't change what's happened. Traveling this land, riding with the herd. It's been worlds better than rotting in some cell or toiling on a work gang, breaking rocks in a ditch. It's not perfect and it's not what either of us planned, but I love it here."

Patrick shook his head stubbornly. "We shouldn't be here at all!"

"But we *are*. I was miserable in England. Aimless. I knew I wasn't happy but had no idea what I was looking for in my life until I found it. Until we came here. Working the land, the cattle. Doing it all with you at my side. It's everything I want."

"Well, *I* should be back home, tending to my horses and collecting my salary, saving for my future. For the life *I* wanted to build in America."

Colin reeled. It was the first he'd heard of it. "America?"

Patrick barked out a laugh. "Oh yes, I had plans. Years of saving to raise my own horses, all gone now. Taken by Mother England, I'm sure. Because I'm nothing more than an animal, not fit to live. Now I'm here on this distant rock."

"Why didn't you tell me?"

"No point."

"Of course there was. I want to know you. *Really* know you. There's still so much you won't share. I never imagined you'd planned to go to America."

"Surprised a servant had hopes and dreams of his own?" Patrick's words struck as if he was fighting a bout.

"We're back to this now?" Colin's own ire flared. "I'm the snobby lord, and you're the decent working man? That's rubbish and you know it."

"I have no idea what I know anymore. All my well-laid plans gone to hell. And what about you? You should be at Cambridge, being buggered senseless and gadding about."

"I'm very glad I'm not." Colin shuddered at the thought of the restrictions of academia, of his family and society.

"Think of what your life could have been. A Cambridge man.

You could have had everything. Money. Men. Anything you wanted. How you must regret opening your silly mouth that night."

"No. I could never regret that, Patrick. I've never been so happy, so…fulfilled in my life as I am here." As he spoke the words, Colin felt the truth in his very bones. "As I am with you."

"Keeping me a prisoner."

"It sounds so terrible when you put it like that. I was afraid to lose you, and I know I was wrong to keep you in the dark."

"What she did—"

"What she did kept us together." Colin closed the distance between them and cupped Patrick's cheek. "Isn't that the important thing?"

Patrick leaned into Colin's touch for a lingering moment, eyes full of regret. Then he stumbled back, pushing against Colin's chest sharply. "No. I can't stay here. I won't be anyone's slave."

"Nor will I! Emily's a good woman. She's going to make it right. Pay us everything we're owed."

Patrick was silent for a few moments as he composed himself. "Mrs. Grant put herself first, and I suppose I can't really blame her when it comes down to it."

Hope flickered. "Exactly. She was in a horrible position. She didn't feel she had a choice."

Patrick's gaze was unyielding. "And what of you, Colin? You had a choice."

"Forgive me. Please try to understand."

"It's not your fault, really. Everyone lets you down eventually. It's only a matter of time. Better to happen sooner rather than later."

"Don't say that. What about us?" Colin's stomach congealed. He felt a strange pressure on his chest.

Patrick took a long moment before answering. "We care for each other. I won't deny that. But there's no happily ever after here, Colin. Best to leave it be."

"Leave it?"

Patrick nodded jerkily. "We had a good run. Time to move on."

Tears pricked Colin's eyes, and he fought for control. "How? I love you, Patrick. I have for what feels like forever. We can have a good life together. I *know* we can."

Shaking his head, Patrick backed away. "It's a fairy tale. *Love* is an illusion. It cracks and fades and turns to dust. I learned that long ago. Should never have forgotten it."

It was as if he was being cleaved in two. Colin didn't bother wiping the tears that fell. "What about everything you said? About trust, about *us*. I made a mistake. I realize that. Yet it surely doesn't erase all of it."

Patrick's face was devoid of emotion. "It's for the best. We were only fooling ourselves."

Although he wanted nothing more than to break down and sob, Colin schooled himself. "Then go. I'm staying. No matter how it was I got here, I belong. I have a place. For better or worse. And that's something I'll never have with you, is it? Not really."

For an instant, Colin held his breath, hoping Patrick would tell him he was wrong. It was not to be. Patrick shook his head resolutely.

There was nothing left to say, and Colin turned. He walked away from the homestead and across the rocky land, resisting the powerful urge to run. He wandered blindly, not caring what dangers he might encounter, and fought his tears.

Chapter Fourteen

AT DAWN'S LIGHT, Colin made his way back to the homestead. He'd fallen asleep near the trickling stream, alongside the herd, the presence of the cattle somehow comforting. As he passed the horse pen, he saw Patrick's mount was missing. His gut clenched, and the reality that he would likely never see Patrick again twisted around him like a straitjacket.

As he approached, Emily appeared outside her cabin. Her hair was only half-braided, and she wore the same trousers and shirt as the night before, along with the same miserable, guilty expression.

"He's gone." It wasn't a question, as Colin knew it in his heart already.

"I gave him his horse and as much money as I could. I'll do the same for you if you want to go after him. Whatever you decide. Whatever you want." She raised her hands and then dropped them to her sides, defeated. "Oh, Colin. Can you ever forgive me? Patrick's gone and it's my fault." Her eyes swam with tears.

"It was only a matter of time, I think. I was fooling myself. It's for the best." Colin repeated Patrick's words but found he didn't believe them any more than the night before.

"You deserve much more than this."

"He didn't even say a proper good-bye. But I suppose there was nothing left to say." He felt hollow.

A door opened, and Colin glanced over to see Robbie leaving their cabin. Robbie made no greeting and headed over directly to the horses. Colin turned back to Emily, who was again fighting tears. "What's Robbie's reaction to all of this?"

"He asked me to marry him."

"Pardon?" Colin wasn't sure he'd heard correctly. Through his misery, he felt a ray of genuine delight. "That's wonderful!"

Emily spoke heavily. "I said no, of course."

"*Why?* Why deny yourself happiness?"

"He deserves better than me, Colin."

"I doubt he agrees. Nor do I."

"Well, he's leaving. As soon as I can arrange for some more men." She smiled sadly. "As you said. It's for the best."

Tallara called to them, and although they couldn't understand the words, they knew it meant breakfast was ready. Colin trudged to his cabin to change his clothes and sat on his bed wearily. The reality that Patrick was gone was still like a dream—a nightmare. That they'd never even kissed good-bye amid their anger and recriminations was something he knew he'd regret for the rest of his life.

With a punch of frustration, Colin hit his thin pillow, sending it sailing. Something fell to the wooden floor with a dull *thunk*. Puzzled, Colin leaned over to scan the uneven boards. His chest constricted painfully as he caught sight of the ring.

On his knees, Colin picked up the plain band of metal. As he held it between his fingers, he imagined its warmth was still from Patrick's skin. He shoved himself to his feet and stormed out, breaking into a run out past the lazy herd.

He ran until he reached a rocky hilltop overlooking a dry creek and thorny bushes. Squeezing the ring in his palm, fingers clenched, Colin pulled his arm back. He wanted to throw the ring with all his might, toss it unseeing, where it could be swallowed by the earth.

Chest heaving, Colin ordered himself to release his arm and let the piece of metal fly. Yet he couldn't. Perhaps one day he'd have the strength, but for now he needed something to hold on to. That Patrick had left the ring at all showed he cared, even if not enough to stay.

With a deep breath, Colin slipped the band over his ring finger, but it was too large. He tried his first finger, where it fit snugly, a constant reminder.

THE DAYS UNFOLDED just as the others had before, with much work to be done. The herd needed more room to roam and graze, especially since the grass was thin on the ground in the punishing heat of summer. Colin threw himself into his duties and fell into bed at night, exhausted. Yet no amount of fatigue could keep him from feeling the void of Patrick's absence, or stop his eyes from drifting over to Patrick's empty bed. He felt carved out and couldn't imagine ever being whole again.

Colin, Emily, and Robbie carried on gloomily. Although Colin attempted to talk some sense into her, Emily seemed set on denying herself a second chance at love. Robbie watched her longingly from a distance and had taken to eating his meals alone outside. Colin hated seeing his friend so miserable as well.

The sun was relentless, and Colin felt the summer would never end. One typically bright morning when he rose, he found Emily sipping her coffee in the shade by her cabin, leaning against the wall. Her late husband's clothing hung off her small frame as usual.

"Good morning, Emily."

"Good morning."

Colin leaned next to her. "You need some work clothes of your own."

She smiled ruefully. "Yes, I suppose I do. Robbie and I are going to Drayton next week. I should be able to buy everything we need there. Give me a list of what you'd like."

He didn't want to ask his next question, but there was no sense in pretending it wasn't happening. Patrick was gone already, and Robbie would soon follow. "And will you be looking for more men?"

"Yes. Robbie won't be returning with me." Emily's gaze remained fixed on her mug.

"What if there's no one suitable?"

"There will be. There has to be."

"Robbie's such a hard worker. He'll be difficult to replace." He was so much more that Colin left unsaid.

"Yes. He and Patrick…" She sighed. "They'll be missed. But we'll get by."

"Yes. I suppose we will." He hoped it was true, but Colin was afraid the void left by their absence would never be filled. Not in the way that counted.

"Do you know what day it is today?"

Colin pondered it for a moment and found he had no idea. He shook his head.

"December twenty-fifth."

"Truly?" Colin was taken quite by surprise. He gazed up at the sun and endless blue sky, spreading over the red earth and dry trees and shrubs. "My family will be dining on roast and potatoes and figgy pudding."

"Mine as well. It's another lifetime now."

"Well, merry Christmas, Emily."

"To you as well, Colin. I'm sorry we don't have any gifts to exchange."

"Next year. We'll have a proper Christmas. Well, as proper as it can get out here."

She smiled genuinely. "I'd like that very much." She leaned up and pressed a kiss to Colin's cheek.

Robbie approached, and Emily's countenance grew somber. Colin spoke quietly. "Are you sure you can't reconsider? He's a good man, Emily. To the devil with what anyone else might think."

Tears moistened her eyes. "But Stephen…"

"Is gone. You're still here. Just think about it. It's not too late. Talk to him. Give him a chance."

She hurriedly disappeared into her cabin. Colin smiled as Robbie neared. "Happy Christmas."

A morose expression darkening his features, Robbie couldn't pretend to smile. "If you say so. Come on; there's work to be done."

Colin followed, and as he saddled up Mission, his thoughts went to Patrick. Had Patrick gone to Drayton? Or was he even farther afield now? Did he know it was Christmas Day? Did he miss his family? Miss home? Colin?

With a frustrated sigh, Colin yanked on his hat and mounted his horse, telling himself to stop asking questions he'd never be able to answer.

His mount was hard flesh between his thighs, thundering across the field, hooves echoing Colin's heartbeat as he flew over grassy dales, splashing through rivers and past church spires. Spring flowers scented the moist air.

Will rode ahead, his shouts of laughter and exultation ringing in the air as Colin followed breathlessly. He'd left his parents behind, their stern faces of disappointment trampled and discarded as Colin raced ever forward.

His stallion soared over a low rock wall and landed in a spray of red dirt. Colin searched for Will's familiar form ahead, but he'd vanished. Rocky formations jutted up from the dry earth under a brutal sun, and gnarled trees replaced the verdant forests. Strong arms encircled Colin from behind, and he inhaled Patrick's familiar scent with a rush of affection and relief.

Patrick nuzzled Colin's neck, his stubble scratching, igniting flames of desire that skittered across Colin's skin. "All mine." Patrick's deep voice went straight to Colin's cock, which throbbed against the front of his trousers.

The horse had become some kind of winged creature, sailing above the land as Patrick lit Colin's body on fire, hands and lips everywhere, tongue clever and seeking. They returned to England and the lush pasture where Patrick had once trained the horses while Colin watched from his window.

Colin straddled Patrick, pushing him back on the grass, their mouths meeting in an endless kiss. Their clothes evaporated, and it was all skin and heat as they strained together in the shadow of the Lancaster home. Rising up on his knees, Colin sank down slowly, taking Patrick's cock inside him inch by inch.

Spreading open impossibly wide, Colin burned with desire as flares of pure pleasure licked out over his body. Patrick filled him completely, and when Colin would have floated away on the bliss, Patrick's powerful hands held him fast.

He knew he should cover himself, that he and Patrick shouldn't be coupling in broad daylight in view of anyone who should glance out a window. Yet he didn't care a whit. Colin felt nothing but glorious freedom as he rode Patrick's thick cock, his thighs and buttocks clenching as he tightened every muscle.

Patrick chanted his name, lips parted, eyes dark with lust as they mated together. Sweat slicked their skin, and Colin panted as he began fisting his cock, ready for release, to shoot his seed on Patrick's chest and face, to mark him as surely as Patrick did Colin when he came inside him, filling Colin with his warmth—

Cold steel nudged Colin's cheek.

His eyes popped open, the vestiges of sleep and the dream

evaporating in a rush of fright. In the darkness, Colin could make out the figure of a man standing over him, the tip of a rifle pressing into Colin's flesh.

"Up."

Dazed, Colin complied, hoping desperately that the dream had become a nightmare and that he'd wake momentarily. His gaze flicked about the cabin, but there was no sign of Robbie, only another shadowy figure who cackled. "Guess we'll let ya put on some trousers. Awfully sorry to interrupt. Looks as if it was a most agreeable dream."

Colin was shirtless and wore only his thin cotton undergarment, which did little to hide his quickly softening erection. As the gunman chortled, Colin quickly stepped into the closest pair of trousers at hand. He reached for a shirt, but the gunman waved his rifle menacingly. "That'll do. Outside."

His feet bare, Colin left the cabin, heart pounding as his brain attempted to process what was happening. His heart sank when he saw Emily, Robbie, Cobar, and Tallara on their knees in the dirt. Three more men with guns loomed over them. As Colin neared, he made out blood dripping down Robbie's face, which was swelling rapidly. Robbie wore only his trousers, and Emily was clad in her long white nightdress. Cobar wore only trousers, and Tallara's dress was back to front.

With a hard shove, Colin ended up on his knees a moment later. His mind spun with thoughts of what the men wanted with them. Surely if robbery was the goal, they'd have at least attempted to disguise their identities. Colin couldn't get a clear look at all of the men's faces, but he recognized one from the day Matthew Barnes had ridden out to meet them.

So if these were Barnes's minions, not taking care to conceal their identities, it didn't bode well at all. Dread and terrible fear twisted Colin's gut. One of the men sidled up behind Emily, reaching down to fondle her loose hair. Robbie growled and sprang to his feet. "Don't you touch her!"

The gunman who had roused Colin slammed the butt of his rifle into Robbie's stomach, doubling him over in gasping pain. Emily cried out. "No! Please, don't hurt anyone. You can take whatever you want. I'll give you all my money."

One of them, a man with a bushy mustache and a jagged scar on his cheek, laughed uproariously. "You bet we'll take what we want, love. This is no place for a woman."

Emily kept her head high. "And who are you?"

His smirk sent a shiver down Colin's spine. "I'm Quinn. A pleasure to make your acquaintance, Mrs. Grant. Happy Christmas to you all. Should have taken the boss's generous offer to buy you out. Would have let you go on your pretty little way, none the worse for wear. We thought you'd have given up by now. We were right charitable about it too. Gave you plenty of time to leave by your own volition."

"Terribly sorry to disappoint you." Emily managed to keep her voice steady.

Quinn bared his teeth in a sickening shadow of a smile. "Came to check up on you a few weeks back, and it was clear you weren't going anywhere. Shame you had to be so stubborn. Gave us no choice."

Colin's heart thumped painfully, and panic clawed his skin. *No, no, no!* He thought immediately of Patrick, of the life they'd never share. Memories tumbled through his mind, long-lost visions of his youth, of Patrick the first day Colin had spotted him from his window seat.

Quinn, clearly the leader, continued. "Now there's someone missing from your little group. Where's the Irishman? Didn't see him through our spyglass when we came for our visit. He gone? And don't lie to me. You will regret it. Deeply."

Colin's voice sounded thin and hoarse. "Gone. Weeks now."

Quinn zeroed in on Colin. "Is that so? Couldn't keep him

around? Your sweet little arse not enough for him?" He laughed heartily, along with the other men.

Colin kept his head high. "I don't know what you mean."

The gunman who had roused him from bed chortled. "Want us to draw a picture? We saw you taking it from him by the river that day your boss lady came for lunch. Gave it to you good, he did."

His face burning, Colin stayed silent. He was furious that an intimate moment between him and Patrick had indeed been spied upon, particularly by these degenerate brutes. It sullied what he and Patrick had shared. He burned with resentment.

Quinn's tone was quietly menacing. "You're sure the Irishman is gone? Last chance to be truthful."

Emily spoke up. "Yes. He's gone. I promise you that."

Quinn seemed satisfied. "All right, then. They won't find your bodies, of course. Mr. Barnes will alert the authorities eventually, properly concerned that his neighborly visit was greeted by a deserted homestead and a letter in your delicate womanly script, detailing how you couldn't bear the conditions any longer. The deed will be left to the boss, along with your little herd. Most kind of you."

Emily squared her jaw. "Go to the devil. I won't write a thing."

Quinn's laugh raised the hair on the back of Colin's neck. "Oh, no?" He removed a large knife from his belt, the blade singing on the leather. He stalked over to where Robbie knelt, breathing heavily, and wrenched up Robbie's arm, grasping his hand. With only a faint whoosh of air and before anyone could react, the knife came down, severing Robbie's first finger on his right hand.

Robbie's scream pierced the night, and Colin shuddered, stifling his own cry. Robbie clutched his hand, blood streaming through his fingers, and Colin's stomach heaved as he watched his friend's anguish. Emily gasped for air, eyes wide in horror.

"That's one. Nine left. Since this one was in your bed tonight, I figure he's your favorite boy. So, how much pain do you want to inflict on him? It's up to you, Mrs. Grant."

"Stop, stop." Emily wept bitterly. "Give me the paper."

Quinn smiled sickeningly. "There. Wasn't so hard, was it?" He nodded to one of the other men, who hauled Emily to her feet and into the cabin.

The only sound Robbie made now were ragged breaths through clenched teeth. Tallara moved toward him and received a punch to the side of her head. Cobar quaked with fury beside Colin but did not move.

Colin was awash in a confusion of emotions. Terror, hopelessness, and a growing rage ricocheted through him as he watched Robbie's blood soak into the earth. He worried for Emily, now alone in the cabin with two of the animals who'd captured them, and who were certainly capable of any depravity. Unbidden, a vivid recollection of the men who'd attacked him on the ship shook Colin. His gorge rose, and sweat beaded on his forehead.

Fortunately—if anything could be fortunate in such a situation—Emily emerged from the cabin a minute later, seemingly unscathed. Still in her nightdress, she strode ahead of Barnes' minions, head high, spine rigid. Although the outlook was overwhelmingly grim, Colin was strengthened by the sight of her dignity.

Emily addressed Quinn. "If you're going to kill us, get on with it."

Quinn guffawed. "Ain't going to do it here, my lady. We're going on a little trip, we are."

Emily's gaze lowered to where Robbie huddled on the ground. Sorrow darkened her face. "We have to stop the bleeding. He won't be able to go anywhere."

Quinn regarded Robbie as he might a dying, squirming insect

he'd trod upon. "True enough. If he can't walk, he'll be dragged. Better sort him out."

"We need bandages."

Quinn shrugged. "You'll have to make do."

Emily took hold of the hem of her nightdress and tore, ripping off long, wide strips of the cotton. Not caring if it earned him a blow, Colin shuffled on his knees to Robbie's side. He put his arm around Robbie's back, supporting him as Robbie struggled to stay upright. Emily knelt and gently took Robbie's gored hand.

Tremors of agony racked Robbie, and Colin fervently wished there was something he could do to take the pain away. Emily's eyes shone. "I'm sorry," she whispered.

Robbie breathed harshly and shook his head briefly. His voice was raw. "Don't be."

"I am. Sorry for everything, but especially for saying no. There's nothing I want more than to marry you, Robbie. Instead I wasted what time we had."

Tears spilled onto Robbie's bruised cheeks. "We had tonight, at least. I love you, Emily. Always."

Emily wept quietly as she wrapped the cotton tightly over the stump of Robbie's missing finger, blood staining her hands. "I love you too. I was afraid and foolish. So very foolish." Her gaze met Colin's. "I'm sorry to you as well. This shouldn't be your end."

Colin fought to keep his emotions in check. "Shouldn't be the end for any of us."

Once Robbie's hand was bandaged as best they could manage, Barnes' men forced them to start walking, the men riding alongside. Judging by the constellations, Colin thought they were heading east, but he couldn't be sure.

In the darkness, they stumbled over rocks and uneven ground. Colin's feet were soon cut and battered, and Emily limped in obvious pain. Cobar and Tallara were of course accustomed to walking barefoot, and when Colin glanced back to check on them, they were trudging along silently, hands clasped.

Colin's throat thickened, and he blinked back a wave of sadness. It was all so *unfair*. He vacillated between fear and despondency, rage and grief. Emily, Robbie, Cobar, and Tallara were his friends—people who had accepted him when his own family had refused.

Still, at the thought of his family, Colin's heart constricted. He'd never even had a chance to mail his letters. William would never hear from him again and would never know what befell him. Colin took a moment to pray his cousin would enjoy happiness and a long life. Same for his sister and his parents.

As they were marched ever onward, thoughts of Patrick returned time and time again, no matter how often Colin attempted to banish them. He knew without doubt that he loved Patrick more than anyone he'd ever known. He wondered at the vagaries of fate—or perhaps of God—that brought Patrick into his life so many years before.

Had this all been part of some plan? That his and Patrick's paths should intertwine and lead them to a new world together, only to have it end like this? Patrick would never know what became of Colin or the others. Would he ever return to the station? And if he did, would it be his doom?

Panic flapped its wings against Colin's ribcage, sharp as knives, and he struggled to fill his lungs. Questions spilled through his mind as the reality of death came into focus. Would it hurt? Would he know when his last breath faded on the wind? Did only darkness await, or some kind of heaven? *Or hell?*

His legs stopped as if mired in quicksand, unwilling to lead him any farther. A rifle butt slammed into Colin's bare upper back, and he pitched forward onto the dirt, pain exploding.

"Keep moving!" a voice shouted from above.

Colin heaved himself up onto his knees. He wanted to do

nothing more than collapse against the earth and weep his terror and sorrow.

"I said, *move*!" This time, a whip cracked the air and tore into Colin's flesh. He stumbled and tried to find his feet as the leather sliced into him again.

Suddenly Emily's shriek filled the air. Biting back a cry as he stirred, Colin turned to see Emily kneeling at Robbie's side. Robbie was utterly still, and Colin's stomach churned. Amid the shuffling of the horses and shouts from Barnes' men to get up, Colin gathered his wits and scrambled to where Robbie lay.

Emily shook Robbie's shoulder, sobbing loudly, gulping for air. Dawn was near, and Colin could see that Robbie's face, usually kissed by the sun, was alarmingly pale. His breath frozen, Colin pressed two fingertips to Robbie's throat. A faint pulse was there, and Colin exhaled. Robbie blinked and came round.

"Shoot 'im now," one of the killers suggested.

"If you were going to simply shoot us, you would have done it already." Colin's voice sounded foreign to his own ears. It didn't waver.

Quinn surveyed them with an emotionless gaze, then spoke to one of the minions. "Sling him over your horse. And get a move on."

Colin pulled Emily into his arms, soothing her as best he could. As they pressed on, the sun peeked over the horizon. Colin's previous urge to bemoan their fate faded as the sun rose, casting a pink hue over the nearby shrubbery and jagged rocks in the distance. The rays of light gave Colin a surge of energy and, with it, an increasing fury that Barnes and his lackeys thought they could simply take what wasn't theirs.

As the flies buzzed to life and the temperature soared rapidly under the brightening sky, Colin breathed deeply, his arm firm around Emily's shoulders as they soldiered on. He resolved that if he was to die on this day, it would not be without a fight.

Chapter Fifteen

THE SKIN OF his back and chest burned in the blazing sun, but at least the soles of Colin's feet had lost feeling as he stumbled over sharp, hot rocks. They were nearing the rocky edge overlooking a valley, and he had a feeling the end of their march was fast approaching. He was unbearably thirsty and struggled to think clearly, his mind sluggish and consumed with the need for water.

They'd been walking since the wee hours, and it was mid-morning now. Colin wasn't sure exactly where they were, as they hadn't ventured out this way yet. It was rockier and much less suitable for the grazing herd. He tried to conjure the map of the property Cobar had drawn to place them, but couldn't.

He glanced back at Robbie, who was unmoving, slung over one of the men's horses. He'd groaned earlier but hadn't regained consciousness fully. Colin thought perhaps it was better this way and that he'd suffer less. Although Colin was determined to fight, he was under no illusions. He knew they were outmatched.

Colin didn't waste energy swatting the relentless flies. He focused on a strategy for attack, although each plan he conjured seemed less likely than the last to be successful. He and Emily neared the edge of the rocky cliff, Cobar and Tallara to their right. Colin's mind whirled as he cautiously peered over the ledge.

They stood over a deep fissure in the earth, a crevasse that split solid rock so far down that the bottom was only darkness. Panic and horror set Colin's heart racing. This was to be their grave, where surely no one would ever find them. He glanced around in all directions, praying for an impossible savior, although he knew it was fruitless. For a moment, Colin thought he caught a flash of movement in the cluster of trees behind the horsemen, but knew it could only be a bird or wildlife.

He prayed the animals would be unable to find them at the bottom of the crevasse.

Emily swayed against him, her chin trembling as she clearly struggled to control her emotions. Colin squeezed her shoulders and whispered. "Let's try and take a few with us, at least."

They shared a long look, with no words necessary anymore as they turned to face their captors. Colin cleared his throat, which was parched and raw. "I presume this is the end of the line."

Quinn smiled. "Astute observation, my boy. Are you going to step off yourselves, or do we have to push you?" He swung down from his horse and took several menacing steps toward them.

Emily's voice quaked. "I'm with child. Are you willing to kill an innocent babe?"

With child? Colin tried to hide his astonishment. He had no idea if Emily was being truthful or not, but didn't hold out any hope for mercy.

Quinn affected a surprised expression. "My word! Well, in that case, you're all free to go."

The men guffawed, and Quinn took several more steps nearer. He held no gun. The other four men were still on horseback. Only two had rifles in hand. It was clear they saw no threat from their prisoners. *Now or never.*

As Colin took a deep breath, the man who'd transported Robbie abruptly hauled Robbie up and tossed him toward the cliff's edge. "Here, we'll start with this one!" He laughed uproariously as Emily dived toward Robbie's tumbling body.

Head down, Colin charged Quinn, slamming his shoulder into the other man's chest. Quinn tumbled back onto the ground, and a shot rang out, the horses whinnying and prancing in agitation as commotion erupted. Colin smashed his fist into Quinn's nose, which cracked in a most satisfying fashion.

More gunfire exploded, and as Colin's fist plunged again, he waited for bullets to pierce his flesh. Yet none did. With a burst of power, Quinn dodged Colin's punch and swiftly flipped him onto his back, reversing their positions. He squeezed Colin's throat, and snarled, "You'll pay for that."

Stars burst in Colin's vision, and he scrabbled desperately with his hands, trying to dislodge Quinn. It was no use, and he thrashed his legs, an elemental panic taking over as his windpipe was brutally compressed and his lungs burned for oxygen. His mind screamed as the black on the edges of his vision closed in relentlessly.

Suddenly there was a rush of movement and Quinn was swept off Colin's body. As Colin coughed and gasped for air, he watched Quinn wrestle with a man who looked for all the world like Patrick. Colin rubbed his eyes and stared in shocked disbelief as Patrick and Quinn tumbled in the dirt, fists pummeling, hats flying off. A dog circled them, barking in agitation.

Colin struggled to process what his eyes were seeing. It really did seem to be Patrick, unless Colin was dead and this was some hallucination borne of his last breaths. Emily screamed for help, and Colin swiveled around to where she and Tallara hung over the edge of the cliff on their bellies.

With a burst of energy, Colin raced to them and lunged over the edge. They held onto Robbie, who was barely conscious from the blood loss, and desperately attempted to haul him up. Colin reached down and managed to grab hold of Robbie's belt. He was sure they'd all be pitched over the side any moment, but no attackers came.

Stones plummeted into the endless darkness of the deep crevasse as they struggled to pull Robbie back up. After several heaves, they managed to tug him back to safety and crawled away from the cliff's edge. Breathing heavily, Colin looked for Patrick.

Patrick and Quinn still grappled together, battling for the upper hand. As Colin staggered to his feet to join the fray, Quinn seized the knife from his belt. The young dog had latched onto Quinn's other arm, but the knife soared overhead, about to plunge downward. Colin dived toward them as another shot rang out.

Quinn reeled back, collapsing on his side in a spray of blood. Still with rifle in hand, Emily neared the fallen man. Patrick pushed himself to his knees, chest heaving, the dog licking him frantically. With a firm shove of her foot, Emily kicked Quinn over onto his back. Blood bubbled on his lips, and he wheezed. Gun raised, Emily spoke. "You and your boss underestimated the *little lady*. And her friends."

Quinn tried to respond, but he could only choke on blood pitifully. Colin looked away. As he peered about, he realized the clouds of descending flies were drawn to the great deal of blood spilling forth from the bodies of three of the henchmen. Quinn soon took his last shuddering breath, and it was over. Cobar had restrained the only survivor and tended to Robbie with Tallara.

Patrick found his feet, and Colin stared at him, disbelieving. He wasn't dreaming. Patrick was truly here. Patrick was alive. *Colin* was still alive. They came together, Colin throwing himself into Patrick's arms gratefully.

He drank in the familiar feel of Patrick's body pressed to his, the strength in Patrick's arms as he held Colin close. Breathing deeply, Patrick's unique scent filled Colin's senses, and he wanted to laugh with giddy relief. *Alive, alive, alive.*

Patrick held Colin's face in his hands. "Did they hurt you?"

Colin didn't feel any pain now that he was back in Patrick's arms. He tried to answer, but his throat was bone-dry. He wavered on his feet, and dizziness washed over him. "Water," he croaked.

Patrick sat him on the ground and quickly retrieved a canteen from the saddlebag on the nearest horse. When he returned, Colin pointed to Emily, who sat some feet away by Robbie's side, equally dazed. She drank from the canteen desperately as Patrick retrieved another and held it to Colin's dry lips. It tasted better than anything ever had, and Colin coughed as he gulped the liquid down. He soon drank freely, draining the container. Patrick stroked his hair tenderly. "Better?" he asked.

Colin nodded gratefully, and Patrick made sure Cobar and Tallara had water before he went after the horses, rounding them up from where they had scattered at the sound of gunshots. Emily tried to get Robbie to drink, and he sputtered but seemed to revive slightly.

The dog watched Colin from a few feet away, wary. Colin reached out his hand, and after a moment, the dog licked his fingers. Its gaze darted back to Patrick every few seconds, always keeping him in sight.

Patrick returned to Colin's side. As he trailed his hand down Colin's bare back, his fingers found the whip's handiwork. He froze. "They whipped you?" His tone was pure steel.

Colin was so numb he'd honestly forgotten. "I don't really feel anything right now. It's fine."

Something close to a growl rumbled from Patrick's throat, and he was on his feet. After a few strides, he hauled up the surviving captor by his collar, the man's hands bound behind his back. "Go tell your boss that we'd better not see hide nor hair of him or any of his men, ever again. You cowardly bastards come back, and we'll be waiting. Understand?"

The man nodded jerkily, and Patrick shoved him forcefully. "You've got a long walk. Better start moving."

"*Walk*? I'll never make it. It's at least four days' ride, and that's full-out."

Patrick shrugged. "Not our problem."

Emily looked up from where she knelt at Robbie's side. "If he doesn't make it back, they'll just come looking, no doubt." She struggled to her feet, and Patrick held her arm as she steadied herself. She picked up the rifle she'd used to shoot Quinn. "And we want him to pass on the message to Mr. Barnes. If he wants to come and give his murderous thugs a proper burial, he's welcome to. But if we see a shadow of him or anyone else near my homestead, it'll be the end of you."

The man was eager to please. "Yes, ma'am. Understood."

Cobar searched the man's saddlebags and left him only with a small amount of food and water before removing his bonds. The man galloped away, heels into his horse.

Emily fought tears as she stroked Robbie's face. "He needs a doctor." Robbie had slipped back into unconsciousness. His wound seemed to have stopped bleeding, but the loss of blood had taken its grave toll.

Cobar spoke. "I will take him to our people. Our healer."

Patrick led one of the horses over and helped Cobar lift Robbie as gently as possible over the front of the animal. Cobar swung up into the saddle and spoke to Emily. "We will soon return."

"Thank you. For everything. Just…please hurry." Tears now slipped down Emily's cheeks. "Please don't let him die."

From his position on the ground, Colin watched Cobar ride away, dust rising in his wake. He took another swig of water and tried to sharpen his mind. He felt as if his head had been encased in cotton wool, and he struggled to think clearly. The dog nuzzled him, and Colin petted its short fur. Everything seemed unreal.

"Can you ride?" Patrick squatted down beside Colin and cupped his cheek with his hand, eyes full of concern. "I'm not sure any of you are up for it."

Colin found himself smiling. "You're really here."

"You'd better ride with me." Patrick reached into a saddlebag that Colin hadn't noticed him retrieve. "Eat." He pulled out a small sack of nuts and dried berries.

Colin ate while Patrick gave Emily and Tallara food as well. After only a few minutes, he felt markedly better. "I can ride."

Patrick peered at him for a long moment before nodding. He looked over to the horses, which he'd tied to a tree. "They seem all right. Jumpy from the gunfire, but they're not hurt."

"Good thing you had a rifle with you." Colin's gaze drifted over to the dead men despite himself. "It was you who starting shooting, wasn't it?"

Patrick nodded grimly. "Picked off two of them right away. Never killed before, but didn't have any choice other than to watch them murder you all."

It was all so much to process. "How did you know we were here? How did you find us?" *Why did you come back?*

"Picked up a spyglass in town. Spotted riders in the distance this morning and saw what was going on. Recognized a few of those thugs from that day on Barnes' property. Knew I had to keep my distance and wait until the right moment or I'd put you all in even more jeopardy. I'd crept up close to those trees yonder when they tossed Robbie and you charged the leader."

"Thank God you were here. We'd have found our graves in that crevasse otherwise." It was still difficult to reconcile with how close they'd come to dying.

"Don't underestimate yourself. You fought back. I knew you would. That's why I waited."

"How did you know?"

Patrick shrugged. "I know you. Don't let anything go without a fight." He stroked Colin's cheek with his knuckles.

The dog nudged Patrick's knee playfully, butting him with its head. "And who's this?" Colin asked.

"Picked him up near Drayton. Well, he picked *me* up, more like. Woke up to him licking my face. Haven't been able to shake him since."

The dog was mostly the same yellowy beige as the dingoes they'd seen but had a much wider face and snout, along with tufts of darker fur on its belly. It nuzzled Colin's face. "Seems like a mutt of some kind." Colin couldn't help but laugh as the young dog licked him. "What's his name?"

Patrick shrugged. "Dunno."

"But you have something in mind." Colin knew Patrick was far too fond of animals not to keep the pup.

"Keegan, I suppose. Little fiery one." He scratched the dog affectionately. "Comes in handy. Can hear something coming a mile away."

Emily spoke up. "We should bury them." She swatted a fly uselessly and gazed at the bodies of the dead men.

"With what? We need to get you all back home for some rest. They brought it on themselves. I know it's harsh, but it's reality. Barnes might be back for more before long. We need to be ready."

Emily peered at Patrick. "And you're returning with us?"

"If that's all right with you."

She smiled. "More than all right. I'd like that very much." She turned toward one of the horses.

"Emily." Patrick paused, seeming to want to say something else. After a moment, he picked up his hat from where it had fallen and handed it to her. "Too big for you, but better than nothing to keep the sun off."

"Thank you, Patrick." She wound her matted hair on her head and placed the hat on top.

Colin got to his feet, slightly shaky but feeling stronger. "Emily, what you told them, about a child…"

Her smile was tremulous. "I think so. I was pushing it to the back of my mind these past weeks. Denying the truth to myself. About so many things."

"It'll be all right." Colin hugged her gently. "He'll be fine.

You'll see. You both will be."

Tallara gave Emily's shoulder a reassuring squeeze. They were bloodied and weary, but still standing. Emily spoke determinedly. "Let's go home."

Chapter Sixteen

THE RIDE BACK to the homestead certainly went much faster than their forced march earlier. Colin wore one of Patrick's shirts to shield his stinging skin from the sun, which was a blessed relief. He'd never been so happy to see the ramshackle cabins as he was when they crested the final rise.

Patrick stayed on his mount. "I'll go check on the herd. You all get some rest."

Emily gazed worriedly to the south. "You don't think he'd try to follow us? Finish the job?"

"Doubt it. He has no weapon. But stranger things have happened."

Colin slid off his horse and winced as his raw feet hit the ground. Keegan bounded over, tongue wagging. "If we keep the dog here, he'll bark if anyone approaches."

"Oh, yes. He'll howl like you wouldn't believe." Patrick motioned to the storage shed. "Should be some spare rope in there. He'll just follow me if we don't leash him." He jumped down from his horse and quickly returned. Kneeling, he looped the rope around Keegan's neck and ensured it was loose enough before tying it to the fence around the horse's corral. "Back soon."

Colin watched Patrick ride out of sight. Moving slowly, Emily and Tallara collected water from the tower to bathe, and Colin went over to help. The feeling had returned to his body now that the shock had receded, and he ached all over.

He put his boots on gingerly, hoping they would ease his feet, but walking back and forth to the tower with buckets of water to fill their basins felt a Herculean task. The torn flesh on his back stung viciously. He sat on the side of his bed once he'd poured his own bath, catching his breath, when he heard Keegan's bark.

Forcing himself to his feet, Colin opened the cabin door and reached for the rifle he'd left propped against the wall. He knew enough of how to use one and prayed he wouldn't have to. Luckily, Patrick came into view a moment later. Keegan's racket died down as Patrick neared, and his barks became playful and excited.

Colin collapsed on the bed once more and drank from his canteen. He was still dehydrated and needed very much to get some rest. Patrick was soon in the doorway. "Need to disinfect your wounds."

It was a decidedly unpleasant thought, but Colin knew it was necessary. Patrick disappeared and returned a few minutes later with an armful of medical supplies. Before the door closed, Colin spotted Keegan outside the cabin devouring the contents of a wooden bowl.

Patrick knelt and removed Colin's boots gently. He set about removing the splinters and pebbles that were lodged in the jagged cuts on the soles of Colin's feet. Dipping into the basin, he washed the skin before taking a bottle of whiskey and splashing some of the dark liquid onto a cloth. Colin pressed his lips together, breathing heavily through his nose, his whole body tensed as Patrick cleaned the wounds.

When it was over, Patrick positioned Colin sideways and sat behind him on the side of the bed so he could repeat the process with the welts on Colin's back. Colin couldn't bite back a gasp of pain when the alcohol met his raw flesh, and Patrick caressed his hair and shushed him with comforting sounds and a kiss pressed to his shoulder.

As Patrick bandaged the wounds as best he could, Colin's eyes grew heavy. "We need to talk."

"Later. Sleep now." Patrick maneuvered Colin onto his side and removed his trousers with quick hands.

"You'll be here? You won't leave?" Whatever would happen between them, Colin wanted to have a proper farewell this time.

Patrick gazed at him for a long moment and then kicked his boots off. He shimmied onto his side behind Colin and pulled the thin sheet over them. Colin wanted nothing more than to press back against him and sleep skin to skin, but he kept several inches between them for the sake of his wounded back.

"I'll be here." Patrick rested his palm lightly over Colin's hip.

Colin wanted desperately to stay awake and find out why Patrick had returned and what it meant, but sleep took him before he could utter a word.

DARKNESS FILLED THE cabin, and all was still when Colin woke. The bed was empty beside him, and his stomach somersaulted unpleasantly. He told himself that Patrick wouldn't leave again. Not without saying good-bye, at least.

Colin gingerly tested his feet and was able to stand without too much pain. He pulled his trousers on and slipped carefully into his boots, not bothering with a shirt. He found Patrick leaning against the wall of the cabin outside. He was shirtless himself and staring up at the stars. Keegan raised his head from where he lay curled up a few feet away and peered at Colin intently before relaxing once more.

"What time is it?" Colin's voice was scratchy.

Patrick handed him the canteen he'd been drinking from. "About four, I think. Woke up a while ago and couldn't go back to sleep. Sorry if I woke you."

Colin swallowed. "You didn't."

"Feeling better?"

"Some. Still sore, but I'll be fine."

"Good."

Now that the danger had passed and there were no distractions, an awkward silence filled the space between them. There was so much Colin wanted to say, but he wasn't sure where to start. He took a breath and blew it out. No sense in beating around the bush. "Why did you come back?"

Patrick took a long moment before answering. "There's a pub in Drayton. Brand new. Royal Bull's Head Inn, it's called. Thought I'd died and gone to heaven. Haven't had a proper drink in an age. The barkeep rented me a room. Didn't even mind Keegan staying with me. Silly dog just wouldn't leave me alone."

Colin smiled slightly but said nothing. He was wary of where all this was going.

"Nice bloke, the barkeep. Talked nonsense, but he was nice to look at. When he passed me the room key, his hand lingered, just for a second. But it was enough to know. Along with the look in his eyes."

Nausea unfurled in Colin's belly. "Is this why you came back? To tell me you've moved on?"

Patrick continued as if Colin hadn't spoken. "I waited for the knock once they closed up downstairs. Didn't take him long."

"You needn't go on. I've heard enough."

"He was down on his knees before I could even close the door behind him and—"

"Stop! You've made your point." Colin turned to go back inside, hurt and confused. "I can't listen to this."

Patrick's hands were firm on his shoulders as he carefully wheeled Colin around to face him. "And I could only bear a minute of it before I sent him on his way. Because all I could think of was you. I missed *you*. I wanted *you*." His smile was rueful. "You've ruined me, Colin."

Colin didn't know what to think. He wanted to throw himself into Patrick's arms and forget what had happened. But he knew that would be a mistake. "You want me now. But what about in six months? A year? You may desire my body, but I need more than that."

"You think that's all I want?" Patrick dropped his hands.

"I don't know! All those things you said—"

"All the things I said were bollocks." Patrick shook his head. "When I was young, I fell in love so easily. I leaped headfirst into it with that bastard, not even looking. No thought to where I might land. I learned the hard way."

"That everyone lets you down. I know."

"Yes. No." Patrick struggled to find the right words. "*I* didn't want to let *you* down either. It hurt when I found out the truth, and that you'd kept it from me. And it terrified me. That you could cut so deep. I swore to myself I'd never let it happen again. I'd never let someone in." Patrick shook his head. "But it was too late. I fell a long time ago."

Colin's heart soared, but he schooled his emotions. "And what happens when I disappoint you again?"

"You won't. It's in the past now."

"I will, though. Disappoint you. I made a dreadful mistake and I'll do my best not to make another, but I'm not perfect, Patrick. Neither of us is. But you just ran away. What's to stop you from doing it again?"

"There's nowhere for me to run. Not without you. I came back to see if I'd made a mistake. And when I saw you with those men, when I thought you might die, that I'd returned too late…that I'd never hold you again…" He cupped Colin's cheek. "Then I *knew* I'd made a mistake."

Colin leaned into Patrick's touch instinctively. He wanted so much to give up all protest. "What if—"

Patrick took Colin's hand, brushing his thumb over the ring on Colin's finger. "Don't tell me you don't want me to stay. It's always been more than lust between us. We both know it."

Grasping Patrick's hand, Colin searched his eyes. "You truly want to stay?"

There was no hesitation. "Yes. This place feels like home in a way I can't explain. I want to be here. With you. Because I love you." His lips twitched up. "In case you hadn't figured that out already."

A little part of Colin couldn't quite believe what he was hearing. He stole his arms around Patrick's waist, and leaned in close. "You love me."

"Aye. I think it started when you told me to just throw myself into the ocean if I was so miserable not going to the gallows."

Joy sang through Colin's body as Patrick's words soaked in. "I've loved you for…always. Always, Patrick."

Their lips met, and Colin felt as if he was floating, drifting away on the night breeze. They kissed tenderly, breathing each other in, touching and tasting. He'd never thought he'd kiss Patrick again, and he reveled in it. But when he shifted on his feet, he couldn't hold back a wince as one of the cuts smarted.

Patrick broke away. "You need to get back to bed. Rest."

Colin kissed Patrick's neck, suckling on the tender skin. "Mmm. Rest is the last thing I want to be doing in bed right now."

Chuckling, Patrick bent his knees and lifted Colin off his feet, his arms locked over Colin's ass. "Back inside with you, then."

They laughed as Patrick shuffled Colin into the cabin, closing the door behind them with a kick of his foot. He placed Colin on the side of the bed and reached for one of Colin's boots, but Colin swatted him away. "I'm not an invalid. You've already undressed me once today. Yesterday. Whenever it was."

Smiling, Patrick ignored him and removed Colin's boots anyway. Colin lifted his hips, and Patrick peeled off Colin's trousers. Patrick's playful smile transformed into a gaze of desire, and he licked his lips, skimming his fingers over Colin's thighs lightly, sending shivers up Colin's spine. His cock was already half-hard and growing heavy in anticipation.

Colin reached down and pulled Patrick's head to meet him, his fingers tightening in Patrick's hair as they kissed hungrily, all levity vanishing. Colin wanted Patrick, and he didn't care how sore his body was. His ache for Patrick was far greater.

Breathing heavily, Patrick stood and quickly shucked his trousers and kicked his boots to the corner. His swollen cock already jutted out from its nest of dark curls, and Colin squeezed it with his palm as his tongue teased the head, flicking into the slit. Taking the hot flesh into his mouth, he traced a pulsing vein with his tongue, eliciting a low moan from Patrick.

Patrick rocked on his feet, and Colin took him in, opening his jaw farther, his senses overwhelmed with Patrick's taste and scent. He sucked greedily, eager for more. After a minute, Patrick groaned and guided Colin's head back, his cock slipping from between Colin's lips. In a few deft movements, Patrick was on his back on Colin's bed, and he lifted Colin astride him, hands strong on Colin's hips.

They kissed as Patrick caressed Colin's body, never touching the wounds on his back. He stroked their cocks together in one fist as his tongue swept through Colin's mouth.

Despite the pleasure simmering in his veins, when Colin straightened up to catch his breath, he couldn't ignore the flare of pain across his back where the whip and relentless sun had left their marks.

His face darkening with concern, Patrick slowed their pace and ran his fingertips over Colin's chest, circling his sensitive nipples. He bent both his legs, feet flat on the thin mattress so that

Colin could lean his lower back against Patrick's thighs.

Patrick held Colin's left hand and took the first finger into his mouth, his tongue tracing the metal band there. As Patrick closed his lips over two more of Colin's fingers, they filled his mouth and he sucked obscenely, tongue swirling. Colin's cock throbbed at the sight, and he took a shuddering breath.

Colin's fingers dripped with Patrick's saliva. Patrick guided Colin's hand down between them, Colin lifting up a little on his knees. He teased the crack of Patrick's ass with slicked fingers, and Patrick urged him on, guiding Colin to his waiting hole.

His pulse thrumming with exhilaration, Colin slipped a finger into Patrick's tightness. Their eyes were locked as Colin stretched him with another finger, and Patrick gripped their cocks together as a moan escaped his lips. "When you've healed…"

Nodding, Colin worked the third finger in. He knew without asking that Patrick didn't allow just anyone inside him. Thinking back to how long it had taken Patrick to kiss him, he leaned down and pressed their lips together. They both panted between little kisses, sweat on their skin even in the cool night.

Colin thrust his fingers in and out of Patrick's heat as Patrick rubbed their cocks together, flicking his thumb over the heads. Sweet tension pooled in Colin's stomach as he twisted his fingers, searching for the little nub that would take Patrick over the edge. He brushed it with his knuckles, and Patrick gasped with pleasure, Colin's name on his lips.

As Colin repeated the motion, Patrick increased the speed and pressure of his fist around their leaking cocks. When Colin rubbed against that spot inside him for the third time, Patrick shook and clamped down on Colin's fingers. He spurted thick ropes onto his chest and neck, still stroking their cocks, milking himself and urging Colin over the edge as Colin slipped his fingers free.

Patrick snaked his other hand down to Colin's bollocks, kneading them together. Colin's release scorched him from the inside out, his seed splattering Patrick as he shuddered and cried out. The pleasure rocked him, and he gripped Patrick's thighs, fingers digging in as he shuddered. Breathless, Colin composed himself slowly and then leaned his hands against his lover's chest. As they recovered, Colin swirled their semen together on Patrick's skin. Marking him.

Lifting one finger to his mouth, Colin tasted their seed. Patrick groaned, and his spent cock twitched. "You're going to have me going again if you keep that up."

Smiling, Colin took another taste before easing himself off Patrick. He lay on his stomach, arm draped across Patrick's chest, his leg settled between Patrick's thighs. Patrick turned his head, and they kissed softly.

"Did you know it was Christmas?" Colin asked drowsily. "Yesterday. No. Days ago now."

"Tried to get back in time to spend it with you."

This pleased Colin greatly. "Shall we have a belated celebration once Robbie is back?"

"Think Tallara can make mincemeat pie?"

"The Australian version, perhaps."

They laughed and talked, and as dawn approached, they slept, safe and sated in each other's arms.

Epilogue

As COLIN SLOWLY woke, the touch of Patrick's fingers across his skin raised gooseflesh and he shivered as Patrick's tongue teased the tip of his cock. Blood flowed to his groin as he rolled onto his back, eyes still shut. He sighed happily as Patrick's mouth closed over him.

In the month since Patrick's return, they hadn't been able to get enough of each other. They slept in a single bed, limbs entwined, and woke each morning with hands and mouths and heated, rising flesh.

When they were spent, Patrick rubbed Colin's nose playfully with his own. "Ready to go?"

"Ready." Colin could hardly wait.

They found Robbie and Emily finishing their coffee outside the main cabin. Robbie waved cheerfully. Despite his missing finger, he'd recovered very well and was back to his old self now that he and Emily were married. "You two going to go do some work for a change?"

Smiling, Colin shrugged. "Thinking about it."

"You're partners now. Better start carrying your weight," Robbie teased. Along with paying them back wages, Emily had made Colin and Patrick part owners in the station. Cobar and Tallara had no interest in land and turned down Emily's offer. They fortunately stayed on as employees, though.

Emily smiled beside Robbie in her rocking chair. "Tallara packed up some food for you."

After Cobar and Robbie had returned from the healer, Robbie and Emily had traveled to Drayton in the wagon and, along with a marriage certificate, had brought back quite a bit of furniture, including rocking chairs for the porch Robbie planned to build. For now, the rockers were on the ground, and Emily and Robbie spent long hours swaying back and forth. Colin loved to hear the welcome sound of his friends' laughter.

Emily walked over and hugged him good-bye. She wasn't showing yet that she was with child, but she soon would. Colin looked forward very much to having a little one around. He kissed her cheek. "See you in a month or so. You'll be careful while we're gone?"

Emily's smile faded. "Yes." She glanced over at the two guard dogs she'd brought back from town. "I'm sure that bastard isn't finished yet. But we'll be waiting for him this time."

They hadn't heard a peep from Barnes, but they all knew they couldn't let down their guard. Colin hoped the man had been scared off for good, but doubted it somehow. "When are the new workers arriving?"

"Should be here Wednesday. It'll be good to have a few more hands about the place."

Robbie put his arm over Emily's shoulders protectively. "Especially since you'll be staying off horses and keeping your feet up."

Emily rolled her eyes. "I'm perfectly capable of working. Not to mention sitting on a horse. We agreed I wouldn't gallop. We didn't agree to keeping me bedridden."

To Robbie, Patrick said, "You've got your work cut out for you."

They all laughed, and Colin felt a rush of warmth as he looked at his friends. He and Robbie hugged briefly, Robbie slapping Colin's back enthusiastically. Colin turned back to Emily. "And I expect this station to have a name by the time we come back."

"I think I have a name already, actually. Tallara suggested it: *Amaroo*. Cobar said it means 'a beautiful place.'"

Patrick smiled. "Sounds about right to me." He nodded to Emily and shook Robbie's hand. "If we see anything suspicious out on the property, we'll ride back and let you know."

Robbie clasped Emily's hand, entwining their fingers. "We should go check on the herd."

As Emily and Robbie waved and rode off at a decidedly sedate pace, Colin and Patrick readied their own horses. Their saddlebags were heavy with supplies, and they both carried a rifle and ammunition. Colin hoped they wouldn't be needed. Yet there were dangers from both the land and from men, and he vowed to be ready.

Keegan ran around their feet excitedly, tongue wagging. Laughing, Colin scratched behind the pup's ears. "Ready for a new adventure, Keegan?"

Patrick chuckled. "He was born ready, I think."

"And what about you? Ready for the thrilling excitement of…fencing?" It would take endless months to finish the job around the entire property, but they'd build it one portion at a time, returning to the homestead every month for fresh supplies and to check in.

"I think we can both do with a little boredom for now. Building fences sounds about right. Besides, we'll create our own excitement." He gave Colin a flirty look.

"Mmm." Colin ran his finger down Patrick's chest. "I think we might find a way to pass the time."

Keegan yipped and butted against their legs, and they both laughed and mounted their horses. Colin patted Mission's neck affectionately and smiled to himself. Although fencing the property wasn't the most glamorous of work, he was eager to see more of the land and spend his nights and days with Patrick, utterly free to be themselves.

Cobar and Tallara waved from the garden they were growing beyond their quarters. Colin and Patrick waved back and walked their horses away from the homestead and over a gentle rise.

"You know, I never thanked you." Patrick toyed with his hat in his hands, rolling the brim.

"For what?"

Patrick gazed at him, intent. "For saving my life. Speaking up in front of your parents, in front of everyone. Proclaiming yourself." He smiled. "I remember thinking you were completely insane. But damn brave."

"It was just the truth. More or less, since I'd only been a sodomite in my dreams."

Patrick winked. "You're living proof dreams *can* come true." He took on a serious expression once more. "I'm grateful for what you did. And I'm happy we're here, even if I didn't always show it."

Warmth infused Colin's chest as he chuckled. "That's an understatement."

"Well, I can be…difficult at times."

"Really? That's the first I've heard of it. Hadn't noticed." Colin grinned now.

Patrick rolled his tongue in his cheek. "All right, all right."

"Good thing I love you just the way you are."

Patrick nudged his mount and moved it right alongside Mission, stopping both the horses. He leaned over and kissed Colin tenderly. "Good thing I love you, my lord."

"See, I don't mind at all when you say it like that." As he caressed Patrick's muscular thigh, Colin kissed him, their tongues sliding together.

After a few moments, Patrick pulled back. "Better get going or I'm going to need to have you right now."

"Not sure I'd object."

Keegan barked, tail wagging, and the horses pranced restlessly. "I think we're outvoted."

"Seems like it." Colin grew serious. "And you're welcome. Besides, it wasn't just for you. I wouldn't change a thing. I'm finally living the life I've always dreamed of. Even if I didn't really know what that life would look like." He shook his head. "That probably makes very little sense."

Patrick donned his hat and took up his reins. "Makes perfect sense to me." He grinned, dimpling his cheek irresistibly as he spurred his horse. "Come on!"

Colin secured his own hat and put his heels to Mission's flanks. He caught up quickly, and he and Patrick galloped ahead, side by side.

THE END

About the Author

Keira aims for the perfect mix of character, plot, and heat in her M/M romances. She writes everything from swashbuckling pirates to heartwarming holiday escapism. Her fave tropes are enemies to lovers, age gaps, forced proximity, and passionate virgins. Although she loves delicious angst along the way, Keira guarantees happy endings!

Find out more at: www.keiraandrews.com

Printed in Great Britain
by Amazon